AN EXES AND OS NOVEL

FALLING
FOR
FOSTER
AGAIN

FALLING FOR FOSTER...AGAIN

KRISTIE LEIGH

EDITED BY
WALLFLOWER EDITS

INTRODUCTION

At forty, I became a divorced mother of one. I had to navigate the dating world for the first time in twenty years, and it wasn't a pretty picture.

After a less-than-amicable separation and an even more problematic divorce, I found myself on the single's scene. However…this shit wasn't for the faint of hearts. Old habits die hard and all that.

People often mistook my snarky and sarcastic personality for being uncaring or detached, but whatever. That had led to the belief that I was a cold-hearted bitch, or so I was told. My ex-husband would probably have agreed with that portrayal. Although, I'd be willing to bet his secretary thought I was pretty freaking peachy, considering I didn't beat the hell out of her when I'd found her face-deep in my husband's lap just days after he had moved out.

Landon and I had met our senior year at the stuffy university we'd both attended. I studied criminal justice and Landon biomedical engineering—just a snippet into how boring that man was. Anyway, at the time, it seemed like a fantastic idea to marry straight after graduation. We were both driven, and the sex was great. Well, it was all right. Decent. At least it got the job done…for the most part.

We knew our careers would always come first and the relationship second.

It had worked for us.

Until one day…it didn't.

On our eighth anniversary, my world got flipped upside down—I'd found out I was pregnant. Not only was I expecting, but I was already four months along. Yes, you read that right—I had five months to prepare for the birth of a *human being* I swore I would never have. That comment probably proves the cold-hearted bitch assumption everyone seemed to have about me but hear me out. Landon and I had talked about this aspect of marriage—we were happy with our life the way it was. We had great careers, we made more than enough money, and I drove my Mercedes AMG G65.

Hot, right?

I was living my dream—*our* dream—but I guess I was wrong.

So, there I was at thirty-one years old and *bam*! Knocked up! I honestly felt like I was being *Punk'd. No one* had an "oops" baby in their thirties…by their *husband* no less. That shit was for young idiots who thought it would keep their boyfriend from leaving. I wasn't worried about Landon leaving me, so I had absolutely *no* reason to "accidentally forget" to take my pill. Damn antibiotics and their evil, birth-control-counteracting ways.

I didn't make a big spectacle out of telling Landon. I didn't exactly *tell* him we were soon to be the proud parents of a bouncing baby. No. I kind of threw the pregnancy test at him as he walked in the door, and it hit him square in the nose. He was shocked and a little angry over being pegged in the head, but I distinctly remember a glint of happiness in his eyes when he realized what I had just shared. He hid it well, but after nearly ten years together, there wasn't much we could hide from each other.

It wasn't like I was angry or even upset. Although, I couldn't say I was happy, either—shocked more than anything. One minute I was cursing my monthly visitor and hoping Dear Aunt Flo would take a fantastic fucking hike, and the next, I was slapped upside the head with swollen ankles and stretch marks. I mean, my doctor had just told me I was going to be a mother in five months. That's roughly one hundred and fifty days—not a lot of time to prepare. I'd hoped Landon would come home and share in the surprise, but that didn't happen.

That was the turning point. When I looked back on where it went wrong—that was it. I had realized at that moment; he didn't want the same things I did. Everything I thought was perfect, he didn't.

We talked for over an hour about how things would change. I was career-minded, and he was as well. Neither one of us would've been content playing happy homemaker—it just wasn't in our DNA. Reluctantly, we'd decided we would both take six months off to bond with the baby, and from there on out, it would be the Nanny Express.

Fast forward four months. Things were a little strained between us, mostly because I was a moody whorebag who was a solid eight months pregnant, and in my mind, Landon couldn't do anything right.

In my defense, everyone would've agreed that Landon had lacked the ability to do anything right.

Moving on.

My life had ratcheted up a few levels on the stress meter. My due date was a little under a month away, but we had scheduled for a cesarean in two weeks. Do the math. That was even more prep time I'd lost. But at thirty-six weeks, there wasn't an ounce of complaint coming from me. The doctor kept telling us she would be a big baby. Every time I thought about that, I thanked my lucky stars that she was breech, and the C-section was necessary.

I definitely dodged a bullet there.

Or so I'd thought until I saw the angry, red badge of courage that would forever mar my lower abdomen, making bikinis almost impossible. It made me question if it would've been better to have pushed the almost ten-pound bundle of slimy joy out of my vagina. Then I'd heard horror stories of women being ripped from front to back, essentially creating one hole out of two. After that, I stopped complaining about the bikini issue and became grateful that I had a scar instead of a vagina-ass. As hard as it would be to embark on new adventures with new flames with a permanent mark across my stomach the size of the US-Canadian border, at least I didn't have to worry about explaining anything before getting busy in the sheets.

But I digress.

When we'd found out we were having a baby girl, I had no idea what I had gotten myself into. I was actually quite happy at that point to be having a daughter. Her room was so freaking cute, decorated in mostly black, white, and hot pink with a Paris theme. The most stunning round crib stood center stage in the room with a canopy and all. It was posh—a beautiful place for a gorgeous baby girl. We won't talk about the mint I spent having it decorated.

I'd given my notice at work, starting my maternity leave early to spend the next two weeks getting everything ready for our little girl's arrival. I bought every gorgeous outfit the county had to offer—or close to it—from Target to Burberry and everything in between. I also sprang for a brand new Stokke stroller and the hottest Gucci diaper bag ever made. If I had to do the whole mom gig, it would be in style. I'd even picked a car seat that would match the seats in my SUV. Because yes, I was *that* woman.

Fourteen days later, I sat in the nursery, holding the most precious baby girl, my beautiful Charlotte Elizabeth. I couldn't have prepared myself for how much Charlie would flip my world upside down in the best way possible.

She became my everything the minute I gazed into her dark-blue eyes. I knew they wouldn't stay that midnight color before transitioning into the beautiful brown she had today, but at that moment, they were perfect, and everything had just fallen into place.

She was who I was meant to live for.

Landon and I didn't spend much time together after the baby was born. We barely spoke. Six weeks without sex turned into six months, but we both chose to focus on Charlie, and everything else seemed trivial. It took less time for us to drift apart than it had to bring our daughter into the world. Before I knew it, over eight years had gone by, and so had our marriage. What had started off amicably enough, quickly morphed into the fight of the century—it could have rivaled *The War of the Roses* by the time it was over. Honestly, I was surprised either of us had survived after braving that battlefield.

After all that, it had taken me years to garner the courage to step back into the dating pool. It had taken Landon approximately thirty seconds, but that's neither here nor there. Even though I'd been seen as an insensitive bitch, I refused to have anyone believe I was weak or dependent on a man. So, once I finally did decide to dip my toe into the sea of men, I'd kept it from almost everyone—it became my little secret.

How things went down, I wasn't proud of it, so it had stayed a dirty secret for a long time.

But now, it was time to tell Dana—my best friend—everything.

"Say that again." Her eyes went wide, almost daring me to repeat myself.

I tried to wave her off, but that only seemed to aggravate her more.

"Kamryn James! Are you kidding me? I've been on your ass for years now to get out there and date, and you've brushed me off every single time. You've told me you weren't ready, that it would be too hard for Charlie, that you wanted to be single for a little while longer. And now you're saying you've been at it for *a year* and didn't mention it? A *year*, Kam." She literally pointed her finger in my face as she scolded me.

"I knew you'd meddle and want to fix me up with your neighbor's son, your Zumba instructor, your friend's daughter's soccer coach, or any guy over the age of eighteen who you passed on the street. There's always someone you want me to meet, and *that* I wasn't ready for. I wanted to test out the waters by myself first. And to be honest, when it all started, I had no idea where it would take me." I didn't want to hurt her feelings, so I kept my voice low and soft.

"What's that supposed to mean?" she shot back in an accusatory tone.

I swallowed my coffee and got comfortable in the seating area of Starbucks. "I didn't plan it this way, but somehow, I ended up dating an old flame."

"Oh." A sly grin formed on her lips, her finger tapping on her chin. "So, what you're telling me is…your past beau started giving you *Os*."

I couldn't help but laugh at her. "Something like that."

"And now you're ready to confess? Why not just pretend like it never happened? You know…spare me the heartache of knowing you'd kept it from me?"

"It's been months since I dated him—if you can even call it that—and I just feel like I'm ready to admit all the sordid details. I'm not proud of any of what happened. I'm actually quite ashamed of how things went down, but as a best friend, I should have told you from the beginning, and for that, I'm sorry. I know you would've been there for me, even if you disagreed with who or what I was doing."

I think that was the worst part about this; I knew Dana would always be there for me—even if it were her brother. I should've told her *years* ago, but I was hoping the saying "it's never too late" applies here.

"Of course, I would be." She leaned over and covered my hand with hers. "Well? Who was it? Do I know him?"

I hesitated for a moment before saying, "It's not that simple. You can't possibly understand how I got to this point without knowing the whole story."

"Then tell me already. Spill it. *All* of it. Give me every nasty detail you can think of." She leaned back in her chair, settling in for the long haul.

I knew she'd do this, and it was exactly what I was afraid of, but I couldn't back out now. She was my best friend, and in truth, I'd kept her completely in the dark while my light switch got flicked.

"I need you to keep an open mind and listen without judgment." My heart was pounding in my chest. I didn't think I had ever been so nervous.

"Kam…now…get on with it."

I rolled my eyes and began to spill the details of my post-divorce "dating" experience.

I, Kamryn Leigh James, do hereby bestow the story of how one of my exes stole my heart and restored my faith in romance, and I destroyed it all.

ONE

IT WAS nine-thirty before I walked through the door after dropping off Charlie at school. I wasn't a morning person, but my one-on-one time with Charlie made the puffy eyes and foggy brain all worth it. Nothing was as hard as sharing custody of your child with someone else, so my weekends with my daughter were precious. It was one of the many reasons why I loathed Mondays so much—not to mention the whole "adulting" thing that takes place five days a week. But we always made the best of it. Like this morning, we'd stopped by Starbucks for our usual breakfast, and then rocked out to Justin Bieber's latest hit with the sunroof open all the way to school. Anything to put a smile on Charlie's face.

I'd managed to secure the house in the messy divorce —thank God, since I now worked out of it. After Landon and I had split, I quit my job and started my own business as a private investigator. When we'd argued over the property, I had no idea just how well the arrangement would end up working out. Thanks to the hefty alimony Landon deposited into my bank account every month, along with stiff child support, I was able to pick and choose the cases I wanted to take. The pay was solid, and best of all, I got to be home for Charlie, which worked out with her crazy dance schedule.

I was able to get a load of laundry going before sitting at my computer to start my day. Scrolling through my case requests, I came across one that piqued my interest. Marissa Sampson. Thirty-six years old, currently residing in Pompano Beach, and engaged to a man she suspected of cheating. That was where I came in…she wanted me to catch him, and if he were doing anything wrong, I'd find out.

Marissa had been very thorough with the information she'd sent over. She included his schedule, which consisted of everything from work to his time at the gym to nights planned with the guys—although I had no clue why a grown man would schedule "playtime" with his friends in his day runner. Other things she included were addresses for his activities, and even his friends' names, places of residence, and schedules. There were attachments in the email, including a photo of his car and driver's license.

Oh. My. God. Her fiancé was none other than Foster Montgomery. "Holy shit."

"Holy shit, what?" Todd's voice at my ear startled me, and I nearly fell out of my chair, but I grabbed onto him to balance myself.

"What the fuck, Todd? Thanks for scaring the ever-loving shit out of me."

He laughed, but that was nothing new. Making fun of me seemed to be his daily entertainment. *Bastard.* He leaned over my computer and asked, "So, what's holy shit? New client?"

I righted myself in my chair and closed my laptop. "Oh yeah, new client all right. I know her fiancé. His name is Foster Montgomery. You should recognize his last name—it's the same as my bestie's."

He raised one brow dramatically, questioning me with a single glance.

"Yes, Foster is Dana's little brother, and apparently, he's engaged."

"Wait, you didn't know he was engaged? Dana didn't mention that to you?"

I guess I needed to explain the whole back story to him. "Dana knows how much I loathe him, so I can't even remember the last time she brought him up."

"Girl, spill. Is he hot? Because the last few guys you've been hired to tail have been dirty old men. I would love to stalk a hottie for once." He rubbed his hands together excitedly.

You had to love him. Todd was my very-gay business partner and one of my best friends ever.

"Umm, yeah, he's super sexy. Well, at least he used to be. I haven't seen him in years other than the license his fiancé scanned over to me. Back in high school, we had the weirdest hot-and-cold thing." I leaned back in my chair and settled in for the long story I was about to tell him. "As you know, we grew up in a small town."

"So I've been told about a hundred million times, but I still don't know where this place is. You speak of it as if everyone's been there before."

I refrained from slapping him, simply because I wanted to get on with my story rather than hear him bitch about how hard I hit him. "Macclenny. It's in Florida."

"Again…this is not new information. Just never ask me to drive there."

"Anyway…" I waved him off. "There wasn't much to do there or many other kids close by, so we were thrust together by our parents and forced to hang out. I spent most of my time with Dana, but there were others we hung out with, too."

Including Foster.

He was always around.

And weird.

"Are you about to tell me you'd go to her house and put NyQuil in her drink to make her fall asleep faster so you could get it on with her hot older brother?"

I grimaced…and shuttered. "Ew, no. And Foster was two years younger than us."

"Oh, even better!" His brown eyes lit up with excitement.

I ignored him and carried on. "He wasn't my type.

Camo and cowboy boots—hell, I don't think that's anyone's type."

"Speak for yourself." Todd was so full of shit. He wouldn't be caught dead with anyone dressed the way Foster used to. I'd be willing to bet he'd disown his mother if she ever walked out of the house looking like she was about to hunt a wild hog while riding bareback.

"Moving on. Foster was always so mean to me. I never figured out why, because all it did was make him even less attractive to the masses, if that were even possible. And let's be real here…Dana and I were quite popular, so he could've totally had his pick of hotties— popular by association." We both had red hair and freckles, cute as hell. "I'm not one to brag or anything, but had he been nicer—and worn different clothes—I might've given him more attention. I mean, I was one of the prettiest girls in town."

"You just got done saying there was no one around. I'm sure you didn't have much competition. Doesn't seem too difficult to be the prettiest girl when there were only three and a half to choose from."

I stared at him for a moment, wondering where the "half" came from, but then decided it wasn't worth it to ask. We'd end up on some bunny trail and never find our way back. So, I rolled my eyes and got to the point. "After years of putting up with his shit and seeing him start to mature *physically*, I completely got over the weird-ass attire and nasty facial hair."

"I thought you liked scruff."

"On *men*. Not fifteen-year-olds," I argued.

"Let's hope not. I know you're single now and all, but you should still have some standards. I'm not one to judge, but I think fifteen is a little young. Don't you?"

"Oh my God, you're impossible. I mean when he was that age. You know…when I was still in high school." I rolled my eyes, unable to deal with him at the moment.

Yet that didn't stop him. "In his defense, you can't condemn him for his pubescent facial hair. It happened to the best of us."

"No, I don't mean the peach fuzz you see on awkward teenagers; I'm talking about a full-blown beard…except with patches that never quite filled in."

"Oh, then I take it back. That does sound gross. And weird. And you snuck out of Dana's room to molest him? I need to rethink our entire relationship."

"Do you want to hear the rest or not?" I was seconds away from giving up.

"Yes…carry on."

"On Dana's seventeenth birthday, she had a sleepover in the converted barn on her property. She invited six of us girls to stay the night and play games. We weren't allowed in there since her mom kept it for guests only, so the fact that she'd let us stay the night in there was a big deal."

"Wait. Back that train up. You were excited about

sleeping in a barn? Did this town have running water? I'm starting to get a *Little House on the Prairie* vibe."

"Her parents had it converted, asshole. It was the coolest place; from the outside, you'd think it was used to store tractors, but on the inside, it was amazing! The ceilings were original wood beams, walls were painted white and adorned with stunning, rustic wood art. There was a kitchen, living room, and bathroom—*with running water*—on the main floor, and upstairs, there was a huge, open loft. It was decked out for comfort; there were no less than a dozen massive Lovesacs strewn about."

"Love *what*? Is that some strange euphemism for testicles?"

"Ew, you're disturbing. No. They're kind of like giant beanbag chairs, but way better. They're made of foam or some shit. It's like sitting on a cloud—you should really invest in one. Comfiest shit ever!"

"Sounds made up to me."

"Nope. In fact, Dana was the only person around who had them. Her parents got them from someone up north in Utah or somewhere. It was a super small business at the time. Now they're huge."

"I'm going to pretend you didn't say Utah was up north."

I stared at him, puzzled by what he meant.

"Kam…Utah is west."

"We're in Florida, nimrod. Everything is north of us. North…northwest, same difference."

"It's a good thing you're pretty."

I glared at him and gave him the middle finger before finishing what was meant to be a short story. "Anyway, Carley had stolen a bottle of vodka from her mom, so we got a little tipsy. Okay, a lot tipsy. Beer was our usual drink of choice since it was easy to get from the corner store, so the hard stuff was definitely out of the norm for us. But man, did we have fun. It didn't take long for the girls to start dropping like flies. I was always a night owl, so I was the last one standing. With no one to keep my drunk ass company, I decided to listen to my Discman and dance around the barn house."

"What I wouldn't give to have been a fly on that wall."

"I'd broken the seal somewhere around midnight and was on my fourth trip to the bathroom when I heard a truck or motorcycle or something off in the distance outside. When I finished taking care of business, I sat on the porch swing to see what it was—considering I didn't have anything else to do. After a few minutes, I saw two headlights shining out in the field, but I couldn't make out what it was. As it got closer, I realized it was an ATV and figured that was what I had heard earlier. Although now, it was silent and moving very slowly. Eventually, I noticed it was being pushed. It came to a halt in front of the porch with Foster standing behind it."

I'd never forgotten the way he looked at me when I cleared my throat, letting him know I was in the shadows, watching him. At first, he seemed startled, probably afraid I was his mom catching him. But as soon as he realized who I was, a lazy grin took over his lips, and his eyes caught the light coming through the front window.

Foster knew I had a slight lady boner for him—but that asshole made it his mission to create misery in my life.

I moved over to give him room on the swing in case he wanted to sit down. "What happened to your ATV? Did It break down?"

He chuckled and casually made his way toward me. "I'm fifteen, Kamryn. I need to be quiet when coming in this late." He sat beside me and then turned his upper body in my direction with his arm resting behind me on the swing. "What are you doing out here all alone? I thought you would be partying it up all night with the girls?"

I leaned back with a sigh, hoping it wouldn't be obvious that I had moved into his unknowing embrace. "They're all lightweights and couldn't handle their liquor; they passed out over an hour ago. I've been listening to my Discman and dancing by myself. I can never fall asleep. I'm a night owl."

He nodded and peered inside, then turned and gave me an odd look. My eyes met his in a strangely fixated gaze I'd never shared with anyone, much less Foster. He leaned in and brushed his nose with mine. My breath hitched slightly in anticipation, but when he tilted his head to the side, he hesitated for just a moment, offering me the chance to deny his advance—like I had the mental clarity to turn him down, sober or not. My eyes slowly closed, and my lips waited to feel his. He did not disappoint. They were soft and warm, supple even. I parted mine as he took the kiss from PG-13 to rated R in a split second.

Our tongues danced to a beat my heart set. It was a passionate, deep, full-on, made-my-girly-parts-tingle kind of exchange. And had the opportunity presented itself, I wasn't sure I could have resisted going all the way with him. But as quickly as it started, he broke away. He got up, and with one last glance, he went back to pushing his ATV. He left me panting like a dog in heat, staring after him while he disappeared around the corner.

"And then you went after him and totally let him bone you, didn't you?" Todd could be the crassest person I'd ever met in my life.

"No. But if you'd like, I could end the story there and let you imagine the rest."

"Nah, I'll need more information for that."

I rolled my eyes, wishing I could rewrite history instead of replaying what had happened the following day. "The next morning, I couldn't stop thinking about Foster and the kiss we shared on the porch swing." Truthfully, I'd woken up remembering the way his lips felt on mine and the taste of his tongue. I had to squeeze my legs together in an attempt to eliminate the weird feeling between my legs. "I'd had the best kiss of my life with Foster, and honestly, I couldn't wait to do it again.

He'd been in a rather annoying, on-again-off-again 'relationship' for as long as I could remember—I use the word relationship loosely as they really just messed around and then fought before getting back together, only to do it all over again a few weeks later. I never understood why they bothered. Clearly, they weren't compatible." He should've just moved on...preferably with me.

I'd been so foolish to believe messing around with me had meant he'd finally given up on the town snob.

"We all sat around the farm table—the rest of the girls looked like shit by the way—and ate the breakfast Mrs. Montgomery had come over to make us. The entire time, I hoped and prayed that Foster would grace us with his presence before breakfast was over. My prayers were finally answered, but it was nothing like I had expected. I mean, I didn't expect him to profess his love but come on. My heart skipped a few beats when he strolled into the small kitchen with his Wranglers and super-fitted tee, looking all sexy. And then my mouth fell open in utter shock when the jackass didn't even so much as look in my direction. Like I wasn't even there. I was so flipping mad I could have strangled him. Who the hell kisses someone the way he had kissed me and then acts like they don't exist eight hours later?" Foster fucking Montgomery...that's who.

"So, what did you do?" Todd seemed far too interested in my story now. "Did you curse him out? Tell him what you thought, and then spend the rest of the day having angry make-up sex?"

I shook my head, not even bothering to entertain him. "The plan was to spend the day down at the river. I made sure I was in the cutest bikini, just in case he decided to join us. I wanted him to see all he'd ignored at breakfast. Anyway, we tied all the tubes together so none of us would drift apart while we lounged around, drinking sweet tea and soaking up a golden tan. The sun was bright, and my eyes were closed behind my glasses...until I heard the shrill voice of Suzie Stanson."

"Who?"

"The skank Foster shacked up with. Although, at the time, I didn't know it was her. At first, I thought someone had slaughtered a defenseless animal or stumbled upon a dismembered body, but I quickly realized that it was Suzie calling Foster's name. I watched as she ran to him and planted a kiss on his lips, the same lips I'd enjoyed the night before. When he picked her up in a hug, I gathered they weren't *off* anymore. Their relationship could've given even the most patient person whiplash."

"So that's the end? That's the alpha and omega of your time with him?"

The details of my senior year continued much the same—Foster feeding me scraps when he wasn't with Suzie the skank, and then pretending I didn't exist in the next breath. That went on until I finally graduated and got the hell out of Dodge! But I couldn't bring myself to share the details of the humiliation that had ensued that year after our kiss.

"Pretty much," I mumbled as I glared at my screen. Gone was the long, grungy hair and the camo—he was downright panty-melting hot. Holy fuck balls, I was in trouble.

This case was personal, and I couldn't wait to dig up dirt on this bastard. For once, I was dying to be there with my client to present anything I was able to reveal about the asshole from my past. There would be great satisfaction in chasing down this demon from my youth. I hadn't been able to catch his interest then or make him pay for how he had treated me, but karma was gunning for his ass now.

I would have usually discussed the case further with Todd, but there was no way I would pass up the chance to take Foster down.

I closed the photo I was staring at—albeit reluctantly—and opened my email to accept the case.

Good afternoon Marissa,

Thank you for choosing KT Investigative Services. We are happy to take this case on and can work within your timeframe.

Our terms are fairly straightforward. We charge a flat fee of

$5,000 for a four-week commitment. A summary of observations will be sent weekly, as well as anytime something important happens. We believe an open line of communication is key, so if at any point you want to reach out for reassurance or to inform us of any changes in his schedule, feel free.

If at any time during that four-week period, you feel the information provided is sufficient, you may opt to close the case. Likewise, if the information provided by the end of our contract does not give you enough conclusive answers (through no fault of our own), you have the option of closing the case or extending the contract at a rate of $1000 per week. However, the fee of $5,000 is non-negotiable and non-refundable.

All details are outlined in the attached contract. If you agree to the terms, please sign and notarize the document. You can either mail the agreement with the payment enclosed or drop it off in person.

Due to the sensitive nature of our correspondences, please be sure that the email provided in your contract is secure.
If you have any questions, feel free to respond to this email or call me at the number listed below.

We look forward to working with you,
Kamryn James
Partner & Chief Investigator

DANA and I had a standing date every Wednesday night. Every week, we'd go out for drinks and dancing, then she'd stay the night at my house. We'd have lunch on Thursdays on my way to taking her home, and then I'd head back in time for Charlie to get out of school. However, this week was slightly different. Rather than go out for lunch before dropping her off, we'd stopped for breakfast. Luckily, she didn't question it once I told her I had a new case that I had to prepare for. Then, I spent the rest of the day trying to calm my nerves, knowing I'd finally get to see Foster—in person. In fact, I'd spent far too much time thinking about all he'd done to me in high school that I didn't once take into consideration *what* I would be doing...until I stood in front of the gym. The one place I hated more than the gynecologist's office.

Todd and I waltzed in at eight o'clock. I tried to stay incognito while Todd greeted—I kid you not—every single person we walked by. I tried to make a break for the treadmills, but Todd grabbed my hand and halted my escape.

"Not so fast, sugar britches."

I ignored the ridiculous nickname and got straight to the point. "You're making it very difficult to blend in. I know you're Mr. Popularity here and all, but we're working a case. It's called *private* investigating for a reason. Otherwise, we might as well be carrying big-ass cameras like TMZ."

He stared at me, blinking dramatically with a slight eye roll. "Blend in? For the love of squats, Kam…you're wearing a hot-pink hoodie in the middle of a gym."

I glanced down at my attire and shrugged. "Ever heard of sweating off the weight? It's all the rage." I looked around the open space, noticing an array of tank tops, T-shirts, and sports bras. "It's a *very* new trend that clearly hasn't caught on here yet."

"Yup. Just like going shirtless under a leather vest."

"What?"

He smiled. "Exactly." Ignoring my confusion, he took my hand and led me over to the weights, which were in the opposite direction of the treadmills.

"Are you fucking crazy?" I did a horrible job of staying incognito when I whisper-yelled at him. "Do you have any idea how embarrassing it is to lift those things? The only weights I can actually use are the little ones, and that's basically screaming, 'I'm too weak for the real ones, so I'm just going to stand here and pretend like I know what I'm doing!' I'd be better off rolling around on the ground and calling them sit-ups."

"Yeah, well, I don't do the treadmill. Do you think my body looks like this"—he gestured to himself like he was on display on *The Price is Right*—"by running? I think not."

I rolled my eyes at his dramatics. "It's just for tonight.

We're supposed to be observing…you know, for our client. The treadmills are up high," I said, pointing to the platform the treadmills were set on, "and have a complete view of the entire gym without being obstructed like the weights." And then I proceeded to regard the machines that kept us from seeing every nook and cranny in the large room. "That way, we can watch undetected."

It was a good theory and completely believable, but honestly, I just wanted to get away from the weights. Since Foster was a guy, this would more than likely be where he would come, but the idea of seeing him left me a little panicky. I didn't want him to see me. Hell, I didn't want *anyone* to see me.

"Fine. We can go to the damn treadmills, but only this one time. I plan on getting your ass back to the gym, and you better believe we'll do some weights. You hear me? I want a pinky swear on this one, Kam." He gave me a look as he held out his little finger.

"Mmm-hmm," I agreed and wrapped my pinky around his.

The fact that he believed he could get me back here was laughable, so there was no point in arguing. Not to mention, by the end of this, there was a good chance he wouldn't *want* to be seen with me inside this place ever again. Win-win.

As soon as we found two machines next to each other, both with a prime view of the whole gym, the front door opened. It caught our attention, but for two very different reasons. Todd practically choked on his drool at the sight of the sexy man strolling inside, while I choked at the realization that I was now in the same place at the same time with none other than Foster Montgomery.

TWO

"HOLY. SHIT," I whispered under my breath.

Todd leaned toward me, yet he kept his eyes glued to the sexy man at the check-in desk. "I take it, *that's* our subject?" His saliva practically gargled his words. "How in the hell am I supposed to concentrate on working out while focusing on *him*?"

"Shh!" I waved him off and began to punch buttons on the machine. I didn't know which ones I hit, nor did I care. With my luck, I'd end up on running for my life on a steep incline, only to trip and be thrown from the belt. Just the thought of getting road rash on one side of my face made me concentrate on the settings versus just pressing random options. "Just get on and start moving. We have to look like we're working out. Blend in, Todd! Blend in!"

"How the fuck do you work these things?" The panic in his voice was comical and had I not been on the verge of an anxiety attack myself, I would've laughed.

"First of all, you have to actually get on it." I waited

until he stepped onto the sides before continuing. "Now, touch the power button. The rest is rather self-explanatory." At least, I hoped it was. Truth be told, while I wasn't clueless how to work a treadmill, I hadn't used one in many years—especially one as fancy as these.

"Seriously, this machine wants to know my age and weight. Must not have been designed by a woman; they'd know better." Todd was worse than me when it came to that kind of thing. One time, I'd asked what size pants he wore because I wanted to get him a pair for his birthday, and he told me it was none of my business. He got a scarf that year.

The machine slowly started to move, thank God, and I began to walk with it. It was a pace I could handle—I walked faster than this to a sales rack at Macy's. And at least if I tripped, I'd have plenty of time to catch myself and save my face from being ripped to shreds on the belt…as well as save myself the embarrassment of being flung into the wall like a ragamuffin.

"Kam." Todd tsked and shook his head. "You can't walk that slow the whole time. You'll have to go faster at some point, honeybun. That won't work." He reached over in an attempt to increase my speed, but I slapped his hand away. He laughed and punched a few buttons on his own machine, picking up the pace.

Showoff.

Todd began to huff, probably because he was pretty

much running a fucking marathon while I took a leisurely stroll. He could say whatever he wanted about my pace, but I knew my ass would be sore tomorrow no matter how slow I walked, so I wasn't about to kill myself tonight.

Foster was across the gym, working out on some contraption that seemed to be better served for torture or some crazy sexcapades—don't judge—I had no clue what that shit was called. I tried my best not to stare, forcing my eyes to wander around the room, only to land on him every ten seconds instead of two.

I watched him move from machine to machine. He didn't interact much with the people around him, completely in a zone while defining his already chiseled muscles. I wondered what they'd feel like against my palm...or my tongue.

He could toss me around a room and I'd like it.

He stuck out like a beacon in the night. His tan skin glistened, and even from afar, I could see the beads of sweat trickle down his arms into the dips of his muscles, as if tracing the lines for my viewing pleasure. Unfortunately, that ended when he wiped away the perspiration with a towel. It had to be the luckiest piece of fabric ever created—no, the luckiest piece had to be his boxers. Unless he didn't wear those.

I had to increase my speed by a couple numbers in order to casually clench my thighs. Just the thought of what he had on beneath those loose-fitting gym shorts had me all hot and bothered.

"Holy shit," I murmured to myself.

But leave it to Todd to hear me. "You really have to stop saying that. Or…follow it up with something else. That would save me a ton of time asking you, *holy shit, what*?"

"Check out his arms." It was all I could get out at the moment.

"You and your arm fetish. Girl, you need to get laid." He laughed, and I didn't need to see him to know he was shaking his head as well.

Foster's arms were spectacular, and yes, I was an expert on that particular body part as it happened to be one of my faves. With just a glance, I'd take in a man's upper body and always wonder if he could pin me against a wall and fuck me into total oblivion. I wasn't light by any means, so biceps and forearms were important—and brutally hot when well defined.

"They're so sexy." Again, nothing more than a thought spoken aloud.

And again, it was something Todd felt the need to remark on. "Sorry. I'm too busy checking out that guy over there." He nodded to the far corner.

I forced my attention away from Foster and glanced in the other direction to see what he was talking about.

"Don't be so obvious, geez." He slapped my upper arm.

"Ouch. That hurt. What the hell, Todd? How am I supposed to look if I can't turn so I can see him?" My exasperation was not well hidden. Anyone within twenty feet of me could have picked up on my irritated words or the annoyingly high pitch of my tone. But I couldn't help it; he was ridiculous.

"Just be more inconspicuous about it. Shit, you do this for a living."

"Speaking of what I do for a living...you're interrupting."

"I'm sure he won't bone anyone in the upper-body section of the gym while you check out the man-candy with me."

Groaning to myself, I pulled my hoodie down more to shield most of my face and slowly shifted to find about twenty guys over in the vicinity. "Which one am I looking at?" I turned back, only to catch Todd staring obviously in their direction, drool practically dripping from the corner of his mouth. "Hey, Todd, you should wipe your face before your slobber starts to pool on the treadmill."

He quickly brought his hand to his lips, and I almost fell over laughing when he realized I was fucking with him.

"Funny...this coming from the girl who's got a stiffy going on at the moment." At least he was laughing along with me. "I'm actually checking out two guys, white fitted-tee and the guy with the man bun."

I arched a brow. "I don't have a stiffy. It's maybe a quarter-chub at the most. And did I hear you say man bun? You're always talking about how you hate them."

"I know, but he's extremely yummy. I can look past it...plus, it would be a great handle—" He stopped talking when I held up my hand in front of his face. "TMI?" he asked with a smirk.

I turned my focus back to the guys and spotted who he was referring to. At least this distracted me from mentally undressing Foster, even if it were only for a few moments.

Todd and I had completely different tastes in men—the ones he was interested in did nothing for me; I liked them bigger, taller, more muscular. Todd, on the other hand, preferred guys who were leaner, more fit and trim rather than bulky and rugged. Although, we could both appreciate what the other liked and were great at picking out potentials for each other.

"I can see why you're so hard up for this Foster character," he said, breaking my examination of the two he had his eye on.

"We're not discussing Foster right now. We're in the middle of your obsessions at the moment. Which I can say are definitely both your type. Now, how do you know they bat for the same team?" This was a regular question, and to be honest, I only asked to ruffle his feathers.

"Kam, we've been through this a thousand times. I'm

not explaining it again. I just know. Okay?" His annoyance with me was obvious, but that was nothing new. "Moving on. Do you think this guy's really cheating on his bride-to-be?"

"I hope so." In fact, if I could get him to cheat on her *with* me just to have solid evidence, I'd totally let that happen. "I'd love to get back at him for how he treated me all those years ago."

My attention followed him from machine to machine while I became lost in daydreams of getting even with Foster Montgomery. Todd was quiet as well, which I assumed meant he was lost in his own fantasies of the two men in the corner. And knowing him, they *both* were active members of whatever crazy scenario he'd dreamed up in that perverse head of his. Time passed as I pounded out miles on the treadmill beneath my feet.

Wait! What the fuck?

I looked down at the machine and realized I was no longer walking. While I was off in la-la land, watching Foster, I'd gone from the pace of a baby crawling for the first time to someone running for their lives.

"You motherfucker! Have you been speeding up my machine?" I couldn't breathe, even after I'd hopped onto the sides to take a break. Seriously, there was a good chance I'd have a heart attack right here on the treadmill, in the middle of the gym, where everyone—including Foster—could see. Although, if that happened, I'd pray for death.

Todd glanced at my machine and then started to laugh. "Have you ever stepped foot in this gym since you signed up?"

I dropped my gaze to the moving belt between my legs, completely confused. "What the hell are you talking about? Of course, I haven't." What a ridiculous question; he knew I never went to the gym. The membership card in my wallet was enough to make me feel productive. Not to mention, it didn't leave my body sore and my pits smelling foul.

"Well, sweetie…you see, you have the machine set on cardio, which means it's going to work your ass off." *Condescending dickhead.* "I don't ever use these things, and even I could figure out that part."

"Maybe I need to come here more often. I didn't even notice I was running until I snapped out of my hottie watching. You'd think the first sign of exertion would be the panting and rapid heart rate…but sex does that to me, too. I guess I was a bit lost in that daydream." I snarled when he began to laugh.

"You know he's a job, right, Kam? And *engaged.* He's off-limits. No touching—I repeat, *no* touching. Not under any circumstance is that permitted. Understood?"

"What about using my eyes? Is that allowed?"

His gaze lingered on Foster a bit too long, and then he licked his lips. "They're free to roam because that boy is F-I-N-E *fine.* Well, if you like that rugged, manly look." His voice was airy and cracked a bit like a pre-pubescent teen starting to go through their changes, letting me know he was in his dreamy state. He was such a man-whore.

"How come no one told me the gym could be this much fun? I could totally come here like twice a year now that I know how many yummy men there are. With a view like that, I could go for miles and never stop to think about it. Although, shedding the hoodie would be ideal, but I really can't chance him recognizing me."

"I'm glad you think so because you pinky swore. You have to come back." The smug bastard winked at me.

Foster finished up his workout and wiped himself off. I slowed down my machine—even though it was pointless, considering I'd remained on the sides while the belt continued to speed along between my legs—and wiped the drool from my chin. Just kidding. Kind of.

Thankfully, he didn't go to the locker rooms when he finished working out, so I didn't risk him walking by and recognizing me. I had let him get halfway to the door before I stepped off the treadmill that had kept me in motion for the past two hours and almost fell on my face. My legs wobbled beneath me, suddenly unsteady on solid ground. By the time we reached the front door, he was already getting into his truck, so I stood behind a pillar on the front walkway and watched him drive off. That's when I realized we had parked too far away to be able to trail him.

Dammit!

"Shit, Todd, we need to put a tracker on him. We should have done that before we went in." I could've kicked myself in the ass right about now. We needed something on him. I literally had accomplished nothing today. Daydreaming about his biceps got me nowhere; I needed to refocus on taking him down. At that moment, it became my sole mission in life to ruin his perfectly ripped, sexy-as-sin façade.

"Don't stress, Kam. We'll get what we need; we just got a little distracted is all." He smirked at me, clearly not as devastated as I was. *Dick!*

"Speak for yourself. I had him in my sights the entire time." We both laughed and headed toward the car. I needed to get home and clean off this sweat before it became permanently ingrained in my skin.

THREE

BY THE TIME Friday night rolled around, I had to refocus my attention on what I was paid to do—instead of drooling over the man-meat I'd watched at the gym the night before. Per Foster's day runner, he was meeting his boys at Renegades Country Bar. I rolled my eyes— you can take the boy out of the country, but you can't take the country out of the boy.

Charlie was at her dad's, so I didn't feel guilty for heading out and possibly enjoying a drink or two. Most PI work came on the weekends when boys would play a little more than they did during the workweek. Which made my job slightly more difficult on the weekends I had Charlie—I hated the idea of giving up my time with her now that I didn't have the luxury of seeing her whenever I wanted. Normally, those were the times Todd would handle it. But not tonight! Foster was all mine.

Nothing about this place appealed to me, but I'd learned how to mingle unnoticed long ago. It was harder to do my job in places like this. Men assumed that if I came in alone, it meant I sought company. So, I tried to find a place near the back with a view of my target and his four friends. I noticed how carefree and young he appeared with his guys, so at ease. They were all crowded around a table drinking beer and laughing at the stupid shit they each said. The five of them looked just like any other group of bachelors, craning their necks as hot women walked by and buying drinks for those brazen enough to approach them. Typical behavior of single men. The only problem was that at least one of them was *not* single; he was engaged. Men were pigs, filthy fucking pigs. And this pack of swine was rooting around in the slop of available women who lacked self-respect. Most of them were half-dressed and practically hung on men they clearly didn't know—in hopes of what? A free drink? Or the possibility of contracting a rare, but lingering STD?

I had to be blind not to notice this was a damn fine group of men—appearance-wise, anyway. I watched as, one by one, women advanced before giving up and shifting to the open floor to join the line dancing. They seemed to ward off any woman who truly came on to them. This didn't get me anywhere. I wasn't making any progress toward taking this bastard down. It was time to take matters into my own hands. I needed to get home and regroup, but before I called it a night, I sat back and enjoyed what little of Foster I could.

Don't judge; you would do the same.

After a couple hours of, uh…research tucked under my belt, I quickly ducked out while Foster made his way to the men's room. I cataloged everything I'd witnessed tonight on my way home and realized something was off. Foster didn't seem like a cheating fiancé, but maybe he was just good at hiding it from everyone. There was a chance he simply concealed his deception from everyone he knew to eliminate the risk of getting caught. By the time I pulled into my driveway, I'd convinced myself he was just a sly bastard who was used to getting away with his affairs.

I hated how quiet the house was when Charlie was at her dad's. Honestly, she wasn't a very loud kid, and there was only one of her. But without her here, the house just felt…empty.

While Foster and his friends shared pitchers of beer at a bar on a Friday night, I sat down at my kitchen table to enjoy a French vanilla cappuccino. In my opinion, coffee wasn't strictly reserved for mornings; it could be consumed at any hour of any day—and when Starbucks was closed, I made my own.

I settled in and opened Foster's file to reread everything. I had to have missed something. His schedule was like clockwork, and he seemed to adhere to it—right down to the coffee stand he visited daily on his lunch breaks. It left no time or place for cheating. I could set my watch to his activities; there was very little variation. Every minute was accounted for. Which meant if he was, in fact, having an affair, it had to be at work.

Foster was the owner of a successful landscape construction company, focusing on commercial accounts. With nothing else to go on, I'd have to follow him from home to worksites. Monday, I would covertly move around town a few steps behind him as he worked. If he carried on with a relationship on the job, I would be able to catch him from a distance, hopefully without losing him at traffic lights or down busy streets.

I'd get this asshole if it were the last thing I did.

FOUR

SUNDAY CAME ALONG with the realization that I'd been fairly unproductive that weekend—it happened a lot when I was home without Charlie for any extended period of time. Before I became one with the couch, I decided to get out of my sweats, shower, and wash my nasty, red locks before donning my Lululemon leggings. Those babies were worth every penny. My ass looked killer in them, and my legs went on for miles.

I was in desperate need of food. I definitely wouldn't win Mother of the Year with the state of my cupboards. While it kept me from overeating, starving my child wasn't the best idea. I decided to head to Target—I mean, if I had to grocery shop, I wanted to be able to buy random shit I didn't need while I was there. Between Target and Amazon, there was nothing left in my bank account. It was a conspiracy against the consumer. Blouses didn't need to be near the milk; it was just a marketing ploy to get customers to buy shit they hadn't come in for—and I fell for it every time. Don't get me started on all the ads that popped up on my Instagram feed...those bastards got me constantly.

Two hours into Target and three-hundred and fifty dollars later, I loaded up my car with a white chocolate mocha in hand—Starbucks was just another reason why I loved the red and white bullseye mecca—and rolled down the windows. With the radio cranked up, Justin Bieber came on. Yes, I listened to him even without Charlie. I wasn't a closet Biebs lover. I sang it loud and proud...haters could hate.

Nearly home, I hit traffic in my neighborhood. As I inched up enough to see what the holdup was, I noticed a dump truck about six doors down from my house that was dropping off a load of rocks onto my neighbor's lawn. The delivery had traffic backed up and severely slowed, but as I got closer, I spotted a familiar set of biceps and couldn't help but stare.

He turned, and our eyes locked.

His mouth opened like he wanted to say something, but we were both frozen. Fuck, he was gorgeous. The honking of the car behind mine snapped me out of my lust-induced haze. The bitch laying on her horn ensured everyone was aware that I was now the one who held up traffic. He smirked, my panties got wet, and I drove off quickly.

I backed into my driveway to make unloading my

purchases easier and then sat there for a few to regain my bearings. The heat of Foster's eyes weighed on me, and now, he knew where I lived. Out of the corner of my eye, I saw movement. Joyce came out of her house in some skimpy-ass outfit to offer the crew what appeared to be lemonade. I rolled my eyes at the whore and started to unload my shopping bags. After grabbing the last of them, I shut the back door and chanced a glance over to my neighbors to see Foster still staring at me. Intently. Trying to rid myself of the desire he provoked, I shook my head and made for the front steps.

I faltered as I heard my name but kept moving.

As soon as I had the door closed, I slumped back against it and took a deep breath. Foster fucking Montgomery, working on my street. What were the odds? I needed to get my shit together. I had less than one hour to get my purchases put away before I had to leave to pick up Charlie. And considering I had basically wiped out Target of everything they offered, I would need extra time to find a place for it all—if I didn't start now, I'd be late picking up my child.

Landon would've loved to rub that in my face.

I conquered the snooze-worthy chore of putting away groceries first and used the task of going through my other purchases as a reward for restocking my cabinets. Purses were BOGO, as well as accessories, so I had gotten a killer coral handbag with a matching tote and two passport wallets. I could kiss the person who invented them, absolutely ingenious; they held everything. I swapped it out—nothing like a new purse to brighten your day. Next, I moved to Charlie's bathroom to update the ugly-ass pink. She had outgrown the girly color, so I'd bought her a chevron blue set to modernize the decor. I sat back to admire my masterpiece and the quick makeover I'd given her space. God, I loved new shit. It was amazing how I could change the look of an entire room with only a few accessories.

I was just about finished when my phone pinged with a text.

Charlie Boo: What's your ETA?

Me: On the way, see ya in a few

I grabbed my pretty new purse and sunglasses and opened the door. I wasn't expecting the knock on my nose that blinded me with tears and obstructed my view of the visitor on my porch. When I started to scream, I heard his voice.

Foster fucking Montgomery had just knocked on my face.

"Oh, shit. I'm sorry, Poodle. You opened the door just as I went to knock. Are you okay?"

That goddamn nickname. Ugh, I could've gone the rest of my life without ever hearing it again. "I'm fine." I sucked it up quickly and wiped at my stinging eyes. "Wow, Foster Montgomery…long time no see. How have you been?"

He leaned in as if to give me a hug, but he must've thought better of it as he stood up straight again. "I saw you when you drove by. I gave the guys a bit of a break to cool off, so I thought I'd come over and say hey…see how you are. It's been a long time. I'd hug you, but I don't want to get you all hot and sweaty."

He had to be fucking kidding. I mean, I wouldn't mind taking him upstairs and *getting* all hot and sweaty…damn, not again. I swear this man was *bad* news.

"That's quite all right. You can keep the hotness and sweatiness right where they are." I backed away slightly.

"Did you just say I was hot?" His smirk nearly did me in.

And that dimple still called my name. It was really a scar he'd gotten when he was twelve, after falling off the roof of my garage. But either way, it was sexy in a masculine way. It truly would be the death of me. My daughter would grow up without a mother, and my tombstone would state, *Loving woman of one child who died at the hands of a dimple.*

I stepped forward, gesturing with my hand that I needed to pass. "I'm sorry to cut this short, but I really need to pick up my daughter from her dad's house." I managed to sound calm when I was anything but. I didn't understand the way this man could melt my panties without a single touch. I locked my front door and took off toward the car.

He caught up with me, and just as I moved to open the car door, I was suddenly caged in. "Wait," he practically begged.

I didn't dare turn around. Foster was too close, too sexy, and I was trying so hard not to breathe him in. "What do you want, Foster? I really need to get going; Charlie's waiting for me." I put a lot of effort into sounding uninterested, though I ended up coming off as a total bitch. I just needed to get the hell out of here.

"All right, Poodle. Are you, uh…busy on Wednesday night?" His voice shook nervously, like a teenager asking a girl out for the first time. "I was wondering if maybe you wanted to have a drink and catch up? It's been forever since I've seen you, so I thought it might be nice."

I sighed and prepared myself to tell a little white lie. "I'm sorry, Foster. I have a date on Wednesday." It wasn't a complete lie—I did have a date, just not the kind I was leading him to believe it was. I had plans to go out for drinks and dancing with my best friend…otherwise known as his *sister*.

His posture stiffened slightly around me, and he moved his hands away, though not before lightly brushing his fingertips down my arms. The sensation jolted through me and caused me to whirl around to face him. *Big* mistake. Again with the not breathing. How would I ever retaliate against him if my body betrayed me every time I was in his vicinity?

He tucked a lock of my hair behind my ear. "Maybe another time. Now that I'm working a few doors down, I'm sure I'll be seeing you." As if he hadn't just rattled my whole world with that touch and his words and his sinfully sexy dimple, he winked and jogged off. When he reached the end of my driveway, he turned around and started walking backward. "I'm not letting you off the hook, Poodle. I'm coming back for you."

As I watched him walk away, he got a text that made him stop in his tracks. His entire body tensed, and I swear I heard him curse. He didn't respond, just put his phone back into his pocket. I wondered what that was all about, but I didn't dare ask.

Without wasting a single second, I jumped into the car, quickly cranked the ignition, and peeled out of the driveway as fast as I could. When I arrived at Landon's, I couldn't remember any part of driving there, as I was in such a daze. Fucking Foster. I got out of the car just as Charlie ran up to me. Meanwhile, her lazy-ass father just stood on the front porch and waved goodbye.

We took a detour for pizza—to kill some time in hopes that Foster and his crew were done for the day by the time we got home. And just as we pulled down the street, the crew passed us on their way out. I wouldn't be surprised if they heard my sigh of relief from the next town over. Score one for Kamryn on perfect timing.

Charlie and I enjoyed our pizza together while chatting about how we had each spent our weekend. When we had our paper plates cleared and the box of leftovers in the fridge, I showed Charlie her redecorated bathroom. She rewarded me with a piercing squeal and then a huge hug and kiss on the cheek before taking a few pictures to show her friends. Her phone rang instantly, and off she went to chat in her bedroom.

I plopped down onto my bed with the dreaded Montgomery file again, and it hit me—I should have said yes. We could have gone out, had a couple drinks, gotten cozy, and I could have proven he was a cheating bastard. I would've won, and revenge would've been mine when I handed over my findings to Marissa. *Bam!* I hoped I hadn't ruined my chances. That thought made me laugh. I knew he'd be back. He'd even said so, whatever he'd meant by that. I just hoped I was right and would get another chance for drinks with Foster to *catch up*.

And just like that, I fell asleep with a new plan forged that would include me being a lot more *hands-on*.

HE JOINED *me in my bed sometime during the night, although I wasn't sure how he'd gotten in the door. I didn't seem to care. Foster quickly removed the camisole I slept in, along with the matching bottoms, before he climbed into the bed and covered us both. His hands were rough from manual*

labor, but his touch was smooth like silk. The calloused tips of his fingers sent chills all over my body. As soon as he laid a finger on me, I took that as the green light to return the sentiment. The room was dark with the blinds closed, but even though I couldn't see his face, I knew it was him. I'd remembered the way he kissed, could've recognized it blindfolded. There had never been another pair of lips like those of Foster Montgomery's were back in high school.

His mouth took mine while his hands grabbed my ass. In one swift move, he had my legs parted and turned us over for me to mount his waist. Even when he broke the kiss, there were no words exchanged between us. I couldn't make out his features in the dark, but I also didn't bother to try. The only thing I cared about was him sinking deep inside me, consuming me, taking me for the ride of my life. But where I thought Foster would take things fast, he moved in slow motion. Rolling his hips into mine, encouraging mine to sway with his. Each time he rocked the boat, I tried not to fall over, but the waves grew higher, and all I wanted to do was drown in the pleasure he offered.

Just as I was about to fall over the edge, reach the cliff, soar to the height of ecstasy, the blaring sound of my alarm clock woke me from my wet dream. My heart raced, but I wasn't sure if it was from the buzzer or the heat of my subconscious. I pulled my hand from between my legs and groaned at the injustice of my inner mind teasing me while I slept.

I spent too much time in bed, handling the *situation*

that the Foster of my dreams had left me with. I quickly realized Charlie would be late if we didn't hurry. I threw on the first pair of leggings I could find and a tank top that almost matched, and then ran to Charlie's room to wake her. Except she was already up, dressed, hair curled, and looking as beautiful as always...unlike her mother, who looked like death warmed over. Thank God for dance, which had taught her how to use a curling iron, because Lord knew if she had to depend on me to get her ready for school, she'd show up looking like a homeless child.

"Hey, Mom. Good morning." She was entirely too cheerful for this early hour.

I rolled my eyes in return. "Morning, princess. It's time to go," I grumbled as I turned around to leave her room. I was not a morning person—never had been.

Charlie had gotten her early riser spirit from her father, that was for sure. She loved messing with me, using that chipper attitude first thing just to irritate me—another wonderful quality she'd inherited from my ex.

We raced out the door, and I couldn't help but cringe when I heard the crew down the street. I realized I had on an outfit that looked identical to the one Foster had seen me in yesterday. The black leggings were clean, but he didn't know that. He also had no idea they weren't the same pair, especially if he saw the neon pink "I need a coffee the size of my butt" tank top that I'd had on yesterday. It was completely mortifying, but at this point,

I didn't have time to change. Charlie's school took the attendance policy seriously, and she hated being late.

When I heard someone call out from the neighbor's yard, "Morning, Poodle," I realized I hadn't run to the car fast enough. I groaned and slid into the seat to start the ignition.

The amused look on Charlie's face did nothing to stifle my irritation. "Mom, did that guy just call you *Poodle*?"

I stuck out my tongue like a ten-year-old and answered, "Yes, but I won't explain why."

Charlie burst out laughing. "Mom, I've seen your high school pics; your hair resembled a little dog for sure. That nickname is everything. Oh my God, I can't wait to tell Stacey about this when I get to school."

For the first time in my adult life, I found myself grateful for the big hair I'd donned in high school. It allowed me to avoid explaining that the nickname had less to do with the afro puff on my head and more with my unshaven lady bits.

I pointed my finger at her and threatened the little brat. "You do, and I'm going to redecorate your room while you're gone. It'll look like Strawberry Shortcake threw up in there. Pink *everything*." My tone was mocking as I used the word *everything* back at her, but she knew I wasn't bluffing, so she didn't push.

Charlie's latest word was "everything." She used it constantly, and it drove me insane. Insert eye roll. I hoped it wouldn't linger any longer than the other word trends that had graced our home in recent years.

With Charlie safely delivered to the hallways of the school, I swung by Starbucks on my way home. I hated that I'd missed that special morning time with my daughter, but punctuality meant more to her than her regular breakfast sandwich.

Luckily, I didn't see Foster when I drove by his job site on my way back into the neighborhood, so I pulled into the garage. I figured it would keep him from knowing I was home whenever he showed up to Joyce's house to work.

I sat down on the sofa with my laptop to type up an email to Marissa. I stared blankly at the screen, not really sure what to type as I really didn't have much to convey.

GOOD MORNING MARISSA,

This is your weekly email update.

Not much to report this week. We've observed the subject at the gym and out with the guys on Friday night. We have yet to witness anything out of the ordinary.

For this coming week, we will focus on following him through his workdays, starting and ending from home.

I should have more information for you next week. Detailed time and itemization reports are attached.

. . .

HAVE A GREAT DAY,
Kamryn James
Partner & Chief Investigator

I REREAD THE EMAIL. I had started to include the fact that he was working on my street, but I decided against that. I hit send and moved on.

I strolled into the kitchen and told Alexa to start my cleaning playlist, and the room filled with music. I scrubbed away while wiggling my ass and singing the lyrics to "Sugar, Sugar" by the Archies. The 1960s song was a favorite of my Aunty Gina's, and it has always brought a smile to my face. My daughter loved it, too.

I danced around, belting out the chorus at the top of my lungs. I did an exaggerated spin and screamed, *"Holy fucking shit!"* when I noticed a man standing in my doorway. I quickly realized it was Foster and nearly passed out from the adrenaline pumping through my veins.

I clutched my chest as I tried to calm my beating heart. "What the fuck, Foster? Why the hell are in my house?" I glared at him. How dare he open my door without my permission?

"I'm sorry, Pood...umm, I mean Kamryn. I knocked and rang the bell, but you didn't answer. I was a little worried, so I tried the door. When I saw you shaking that ass and singing, I couldn't help but watch the show." His tone was soft and meek, much like that of a scolded child. *Shit.*

I told Alexa to turn off and grabbed a bottle of water before I hopped up on the island, trying to act casual. If it were any other man, I'm sure I wouldn't have been so forgiving. Although I disliked him, it was Foster, and I couldn't help myself when I was around him. "It's okay. Thanks for checking on me, but don't let it happen again." I warned. "So, uh…what's up?" Again, I tried to sound nonchalant. Not sure it worked this time, either.

"I wanted to see if you were up for lunch. There's a really great burger place around the corner." His sad eyes and weak smile made him look hopeful.

I stared down at myself and cringed, realizing I still hadn't changed clothes—at least my panties were clean. Just kidding; I didn't wear them anymore. Yep, I'd turned a new leaf a few years back and decided to chuck all my underwear. I didn't own a single pair and had zero regrets.

"I'm sorry, that sounds great, but as you can see, I'm not dressed to go out. I was in a rush this morning to get Charlie to school and grabbed the first thing I saw…so I'm not quite presentable enough to go out."

He looked me up and down with a grin and said, "I don't mind waiting while you get ready."

I hesitated for a moment before putting down my bottle and jumped off the counter. "Are you sure? I'll try to be quick."

Foster stepped forward and smacked me on the ass. "Get moving; I'm starving."

I yelped and rubbed my bottom while I scurried up the stairs. Although I was shocked at his forwardness, I think I liked that a little too much.

After turning on the shower, I stripped down and got in. I cleaned my face and then quickly washed my hair. As I cleansed my body, I skimmed over my breasts, my nipples on high alert, and super sensitive. The slight brush of my hand sent a shiver through my body directly to my pussy. I hadn't been this turned on in years, and all Foster had done was smack my ass. I couldn't think of a time anyone had ever done that to me. I worked the lather over my body, and when I made it down to the apex of my thighs, I couldn't help the circle my fingers made around my clit. I closed my eyes to envision what it would feel like to have Foster's massive hands all over me. My fingers continued to play between my legs while my free hand tugged at my nipple. The pain surprisingly heightened the pleasure building in my body. I grabbed the showerhead, quickly changed the setting, and sat on the tiled bench. I positioned the stream of warm water right where I needed it and let out a loud moan. I was so worked up that I couldn't think straight. I inserted two fingers and thrust upward while the pulsing of the water continued to drive me higher. Panting and moaning while my body reached new heights, I climaxed for the second time in one day while thinking of Foster.

I stood on jelly legs with an enormous grin on my face. I finished washing up and stepped out to towel off. There was no time to do anything with my hair, so I threw it into a messy bun atop my head and brushed my teeth. Once in the bedroom, I pulled on my favorite pair of worn jeans, a faded Roxy tee, and my new converse ballet flats before heading downstairs. Halfway down, it hit me. I hadn't even attempted to be quiet—and shit, I'd more than likely called out his name. The house had thin walls, and while I hoped he hadn't heard me, chances were good that he had. The heat in my cheeks, I'm sure, resembled a sunburn, as I knew they had flamed red, but I walked down with my head held high. I rounded the corner to find Foster on the phone. Thank God, maybe he was too busy with his call to have heard me.

When he turned, he skimmed me from head to toe, winked, and then smirked. Fuck, he knew. Motioning for us to go, I grabbed my purse. Foster followed me out the door and disconnected his call. He put his arm around my neck like he was about to give me a noogie, but instead, he whispered into my ear, "How was it?" and kissed my cheek.

Embarrassment took over, but I didn't pull away, fearing the look in his eyes. Rather than reward him with either the denial or humiliation he likely expected, I respond with, "So good, Foster. So fucking good."

I followed Foster to his massive, lifted truck. I couldn't speak for anyone else, but I had a thing for sexy men in big-ass trucks. So rugged and...mmm. It was high enough that Foster took it upon himself to hoist me up by my waist. The tingles that had become familiar when he was around raced to the juncture between my thighs. My body seriously needed to stop reacting to him this way. He jumped in the driver's seat, and we arrived at Grease Burger Bar in fifteen minutes.

"I've never been here. I've driven by it so many times, but I've never had the chance to stop in. Can't wait to try it out." My feet hit the ground before Foster could get to my side and touch me again. But that didn't stop him.

He placed his hand at the small of my back. I knew this meant nothing to him, but the electricity I felt when he touched me had always been there, ever since we were kids...and it still was.

The hostess seated us while blatantly checking out Foster. Bitch. Couldn't she see he was with someone—*never mind the fact that I wasn't his fiancée*, I thought to myself. Foster ordered for me, and we sat in silence for a bit while I fiddled with the napkin under my soda.

"So, what's new, Poodle? How's Charlie? Work? Everything? It's been so long since we've talked. I hear bits and pieces from Dana, but I would love to hear from you." From the sounds of it, he was genuinely interested. I looked up to find him looking at me as he waited for my response.

It was odd to sit there and act as if we were old

friends when he'd done nothing but torment me in my youth. The constant back and forth whenever he wasn't fucking around with Suzie had done a number on my self-esteem, which took years to recover from. But here we sat as if we didn't share a shaky past. Thinking of it only being in the past made me laugh because that would mean it was over. And it most certainly was not. After all, he was the subject for a case I'd been hired for, although that didn't stop me from wanting to devour him and justify it as business-related.

I. Was. Losing. My. Mind. There's no way I could sleep with him and not completely ruin my reputation.

We made small talk throughout the meal, and I found it difficult to remember why he'd been such a pain in my ass during high school. The immature antics seemed to have vanished, and an adult version of the man I'd wished he would have been now sat before me. It was easy to forget why I was here and what I had set out to accomplish. But with each minute that passed, I grew fonder of the man in front of me. Everything felt so natural with him—when he'd held my hand or patted my ass, I hadn't thought of anything but him, and my libido was off the charts. The playful banter only served to arouse me more and further confused my mission.

Foster and I were in the middle of laughing over some childhood memories when his phone flashed on the table with an unknown name.

Unknown: We need to talk. You can't ignore me forever.

Foster's demeanor changed immediately. His posture grew rigid, and his expression became blank. He didn't respond, just shut off his phone. I asked him if everything was okay, but he just smiled and pretended like it was fine. The rest of the lunch was still comfortable, though things felt off.

When we got back to my house, he let me out, but not before laying a long and heavy kiss on my lips. It reminded me of the one I'd received so many years ago, but this time, there'd been no alcohol to induce it. Truth be told, I would've been powerless to stop it had he not insisted he had to return to the job site.

"Do you have plans tonight?" he asked before I closed the door. The hopeful glint in his eyes almost had me begging him to come inside.

"No, but Charlie will be home." I couldn't stop the melancholy from invading my tone. I saw his disappointment and offered another solution. "But you could come by after she goes to bed if you'd like. We could hang out. Maybe watch a movie?" This was a dangerous game to play. I knew how easily my feelings could get involved, and that could get messy. My client —and subsequent case—had to remain my top priority. Prove he was a cheating bastard, get my revenge, and be done.

Wow. My logic didn't even sound reasonable to me. But stupidly, I wanted to work in an orgasm or two in between.

"Sounds good. What's your number?" If his satisfied grin weren't so damn sexy, I'd wipe it off his face with swift rejection.

I rattled off the digits, and he quickly sent me a text.

"Just let me know when you're ready, and I'll head over. I don't live far from here."

I waved as I closed the door behind me and prayed I could keep this professional. Who was I kidding? After that dream I'd had, as well as my shower earlier, and the kiss to top it off, I needed to find out if he was as good as my imagination indicated he was. I just had to make sure my heart remained detached.

Trying to keep myself busy proved to be worthless. My mind was all over the place with thoughts of Foster, and no matter what I did, I couldn't shake him from my daydreams, which had become fantasies that, after a while, had developed into very detailed plans for the evening.

I snapped out of my reverie when I heard a knock at the door, quickly followed by the subtle creak of the hinges as it opened and closed. I glanced up to find Todd stalking toward me, his lips pinched in an odd half-smirk, half-scowl as if he fought hard to keep a straight face.

"You whore!" He held back a smile and tried to sound stern.

"What the fuck, Todd?" I was at a loss as to why he'd decided to call me a whore. There was no way he knew what had gone through my head all day.

"Oh, don't you play dumb with me. I saw you having lunch with our 'client' today." He used air quotes, which was his way of calling me out—something he picked up from a movie, no doubt. *Shit.*

"It was just lunch, geez. Take a chill pill," I said with over-the-top dramatics to match his.

"Oh, puh-lease, bitch. Drop the act; we both know your ass is far from innocent. I want deets. What happened?" He went from accusing to excited in three-point-five seconds.

"He came over and asked if I wanted to go to lunch, and I accepted. I think a more hands-on approach would be best with this case." I shrugged like it was no big deal.

He raised his brows. "Is that so? How hands-on are we talking?"

"Honestly, as hands-on as it takes." I wasn't willing to let him in on my real plans. For many completely obvious reasons, I doubted he'd be on board with that. Just a hunch.

"You're sure about this, Kami? You know I'll back you one hundred percent; I just want to make sure you've thought everything through."

"Aw." I pinched his cheek. "Is Toddey Woddey all

concerned for Kami Wammy?" It wouldn't be the first time I'd had to get involved in a case, but this time it would be personal.

He shook his head out of my grasp and frowned. "Really? I just want to make sure you know what you're doing."

I sighed, moving to the couch in defeat. "I know, and I appreciate that, but I'm willing to do anything to nail Foster to the wall for how he treated me back in the day." The last part came out a little angrier than I had intended.

He sighed as he walked toward me. "Okay, okay. I get it." He put his hands up in surrender and then came over to sit beside me on the sofa. "So, when are we seeing him next?"

"Not sure…we exchanged numbers, though. That'll make things easier." A little white lie wouldn't hurt anyone.

"Just double-checking here, so don't bite my head off, but you're still in agreement that it's unethical to engage in anything legitimately physical with him…right?"

I rolled my eyes and waved him off. "Please, Todd. I don't know how you do things, but around here, exchanging phone numbers doesn't equate to having sex. And besides, it wouldn't be the first time I skated the line on ethics to bring a client some closure. I'd be doing her a favor in the long run."

"Like I said…I was simply making sure we were still

on the same page. What's your plan, anyway? Wait to see if he contacts you?"

We chatted a little more about Foster and how I planned to catch him—most of it was bullshit, mind you; he didn't need to know *everything*. When I could no longer make anything else up, I decided to change the subject by asking, "How are things with the guys from the gym?"

His face lit up as he pulled himself to his feet. "Oh shit, girl! I didn't tell you? So yesterday, when I was at the gym, Jeff was there."

I frantically waved my hands in the air to interrupt. "Wait, is this man bun or fitted-tee guy?"

He shook his head in dismay but carried on. "Man bun. Anyway, I decided to make my move, so I went up to him and said, 'I can think of at least two other ways to burn a lot more calories.' He busted out laughing, and it was all smooth sailing from there. We made a date for coffee tomorrow."

"Oh my God, that's so cheesy." I couldn't stop laughing, but only because of his antics. I truly loved it when Todd started to date someone. He gave me all the juicy details without leaving out anything. "I can't believe it worked. I'm so excited for you."

"But wait, it gets better. When I was leaving the gym, on the way out to my car, I literally bumped into Ryan— fitted-tee guy. He wasn't paying attention and ran right into me. His phone went flying, and I caught it mid-air."

"Shut up. And? What happened?"

"We talked for a minute, and just as I was about to get into my car, he asked me if I wanted to have coffee with him on Tuesday. Looks like I'm having coffee with both hotties tomorrow. Can you fucking believe that shit?"

"Yes, I can absolutely believe that shit; look at you."

He did a little turn. "Very true; I am quite irresistible." He flopped down onto the sofa in a dramatic fashion and sighed dreamily. "I can't wait. Tomorrow's going to be one hell of a day."

"I bet."

Charlie waltzed in the front door. I let her walk home with her friend, Tiffany, who lived down the street. I didn't usually let her do that, but Tiffany's mom, Jessica, secretly followed the girls until they reached the neighborhood, and then she went around the other way to beat her daughter home. So, I was okay with them walking with a chaperone.

"Hey, Mom," Charlie yelled from the foyer.

"Hi, honey. We're in here."

Todd jumped up off the sofa and nearly knocked Charlie on her ass when she came into the living room. He picked her up and hugged her tight. She was in a fit of laughter by the time he set her down. "How's my favorite girl?"

"I'm good, how are you, Uncle Todd?" She'd referred to him as her uncle for quite some time now. He was one of her favorite people in the world; plus, Todd was an amazing shopping partner and usually sided with Charlie when we argued.

"Fabulous. Would you expect anything less?" He gave her an expressive "duh" face, which brought on more laughter. "How's dance? When's the next time I get to throw flowers on a stage for you? I hope soon because that was fun."

She propped her fist on her hip that she had jutted out, for nothing other than to entertain his dramatic flair. "I'm not telling you if you're going to do that again. You're either supposed to hand it to the dancer, or carefully set the bouquets on the edge of the stage. They aren't baseballs, and not meant to be *thrown* at us."

"It's not my fault if you didn't catch them. And in my defense, I made sure they didn't have thorns first. You should be thanking me."

"Speaking of dance..." I piped in, knowing I wouldn't get a word in edgewise between these two if I didn't make room. "Charlie, you have to get ready. We have to leave soon to pick up Kaylie."

Kaylie was in Charlie's dance company, and I'd grown close with her mother over the last few years of the girls being in ballet together. Ever since I'd started my own business—and had to deal with the back and forth with Landon—Jenny, Kaylie's mom, had offered to carpool; I'd drive the girls to the studio, and she'd bring them home. The only times we'd switch things up were during "hell week." That was what we called the brutal practices right before a major competition, when the girls had long hours in the studio, perfecting the choreography. During those days, Jenny and I sat in a quiet corner with a thermos of coffee and chatted until the girls dragged us out.

"Oh, I totally forgot to ask, Mom." Translation: *I waited until the last minute because I didn't want you to say no.* She thought she was sneaky, but I knew *all* the tricks—because I still held them up my sleeve. "Kaylie had invited me to sleepover at her house tonight."

"On a school night?"

"Well, if tonight's a school night…then yeah."

I rolled my eyes at her sarcasm, while Todd held a fisted hand to his mouth to keep from laughing out loud. This wasn't his first rodeo. He knew if she'd caught him with so much as a smirk, she'd win, and that meant he'd lose because I'd kick his ass.

"C'mon, Mom," she whined—which never got her anywhere, although now that I had plans this evening, it quite possibly could get her everywhere. "We have a group paper for class, and she's my writing buddy. We were supposed to do it this weekend, but Dad wouldn't take me over there, and he said she wasn't allowed at the house."

That didn't surprise me. Jenny was Team Kam all the way—head cheerleader, captain of the squad, and offensive *and* defensive coach. I just hated how Landon managed to punish his own daughter simply because he detested the girl's mother. It wasn't Charlie's fault that her friends' moms were smart and sided with the right person.

"When's this paper due?"

"Friday."

I groaned. That meant there wouldn't be any other time for her to get it done. She went to her dad's house every Wednesday, so if she didn't get it done tonight, that would put both girls scrambling at the last minute to complete the assignment. Despite my own procrastination issues, I didn't need my daughter suffering from it, too.

"And you can't do it in class?"

She looked to Todd—which meant she had plenty of time to finish it in class.

My very smart business partner held up his hands in surrender. "Sorry, kiddo, but this isn't my call. You know if I made the decisions around here, I'd tell you to go pack a bag and not stay up too late tonight." Well, maybe he wasn't as smart as I'd thought.

"Gee, thanks, Todd." I glared at him and then ignored his *"what'd I do?"* head bob. Turning my attention back to the little human who'd inherited all my charm and none of my slyness, I added, "Let me call Jenny."

"Oh, she already said she was okay with it if you were." She'd learned far too many bad things from the man snickering beside me.

"How about I call her to verify that."

"Would you look at the time… I need to get going. I just stopped by to pester your mom about something. Have fun at dance." He squeezed her tightly and then turned to me. "And I'll see you bright and early in the morning." He kissed us both goodbye before practically skipping out of the house.

Jenny was quick to answer—got to love the ones who always had their phone on and didn't make people wait for eons for a response—and to my surprise, Charlie was right. She didn't have a problem with the girls staying over at her house to finish an assignment, and then added in a few choice words regarding Landon. Those put a smile on my face. Then she apologized for forgetting to mention this earlier—apparently, it had been planned since yesterday.

As much as I didn't want to lose yet another night this week with Charlie—Wednesdays were bad enough —I didn't want my own selfishness to interfere with her grades. Plus, this now gave me more time and freewill to hammer as many nails into Foster's coffin as I could. Technically, he would be the one doing the hammering if he played his cards right.

ONCE HOME from dropping the girls off at dance, I jumped into the shower. There was no guarantee of how the night would go, but any smart woman would prepare for everything and anything. So, I took my time shaving my legs. Too bad I didn't have more notice; otherwise, I would've made an appointment at the salon to freshen up my bikini line. Instead, I was left to tend to that myself. If I had my way, he'd never remember the nickname "Poodle" again. After tonight, he'd call me Mr. Bigglesworth. No…just no. I needed to think of something better—although the idea of his petting me the way Dr. Evil stroked his hairless cat made me desperate for him—Foster, not Mike Myers.

After I triple checked every inch of me to make sure there was no hair left unshaven, I dried off, lathered my body in expensive lotion—it toned *and* moisturized, something Todd's gym couldn't do—and then rummaged through my drawers for an outfit that didn't look like I'd spent any time on it. The key was to look comfortable without appearing homeless. Foster didn't need to know the lengths I'd gone to tonight.

With my hair completely dried and styled to look like I hadn't taken any effort whatsoever on it, I grabbed my phone and sent him a text.

Me: You can head over in about 30 mins

Foster: See you soon

The beam of headlights flashed through the front window as Foster pulled in to the driveway. My stomach was in knots, and the longer he waited without knocking on the door, the worse it got. Peeking through the blinds, I noticed that he sat in his truck, but he hadn't gotten out. I couldn't imagine what he would be doing. Suddenly, my cell vibrated in my hand, and a loud ping rang out through the room, startling me half to death. I nearly jumped out of my seat—and the abrupt movement more than likely alerted him to my spying.

Checking the screen on my phone, I noticed it was a text from Foster.

Foster: I'm here, is the coast clear?

Me: Ha! Yes, Charlie is at a sleepover

The bubbles seemed to go on forever before another message popped up.

Foster: ;) OK then, coming in

Me: OK

I opened the door and waited for him like a greeter at Victoria's Secret. My confidence was solid…until he stepped out of his truck and paused with his hand on the door as if he were frozen in the midst of closing it. Even with the distance between us and the sky dusky from the sunset, I could clearly see him rake his gaze over me from head to toe.

Oh, boy…this man was trouble. He looked sexy as

hell in his low-slung jeans and fitted, white Henley. And when he stalked toward me, his swagger alone nearly had me on the cusp of an orgasm. No other gait in the history of walking had ever turned me on as much as Foster's did right now.

I welcomed him in and grabbed the popcorn from the kitchen, hoping he wouldn't pick up on my intense desire to sit on his face. We each took a seat on the couch and flipped through the movie options On Demand, settling on *Knocked Up*. If you expected me to pick some crap like *The Notebook*, you clearly haven't been paying attention to my motivation. I had no intention of crying on his shoulder—nothing killed a libido quite like Nicholas Sparks. If I planned to get anything out of this, I needed comedy and a hint of sex. Not to mention, laughing your ass off yielded many opportunities to touch someone in a playful way, and any woman who knew what she was doing could turn teasing touches into sensual caresses. And once you got a guy there, you were about two seconds from having his wood in your fireplace.

I tried to watch the movie—not really, but at least I pretended to—while Foster wasted no time getting cozy with his hand on my upper thigh. I had on loose-fitting cotton shorts that put him quite close to the throbbing ache between my legs. He had me all hot and bothered in seconds; it took far too much effort to keep from squirming. So much for my getting him all hot and bothered. He turned the tables with the simple touch on my thigh. I didn't doubt he could hear me panting or that he could feel me clench my thighs to relieve the pulsating need that he'd put there with one little stroke of his finger against my flesh. As if that weren't bad enough, he began to rub small circles with his thumb while slowly inching closer to where I so desperately wanted him. I swallowed hard and nonchalantly glanced down to see how affected he was by this as well. My eyes practically bugged out of my head when I noticed his massive erection straining against the fly of his jeans, just begging to come out and play.

I turned my head to the left at the same time Foster shifted to face me. He stared at me for a moment, silently asking permission, and that thin, worn-out rubber band that had restrained me ever since seeing him that night at the gym snapped. I launched myself at him and devoured his mouth while I straddled his hips. Foster quickly took control of the kiss. His rough hands grazed my sensitive flesh as they slid up my thighs, and then he roughly palmed my ass, squeezing hard until I was sure he'd left marks that would linger for days. I groaned out my pleasure, surprised to hear such a carnal sound coming from my chest. Being manhandled wasn't new to me, but seeing as I'd been with Landon for so long, it was always a nice surprise when a man took control and showed a little roughness...or a lot.

I ground down on Foster's erection, trying to ease

some of the pressure that continued to build. He apparently liked that, because he growled—yes, growled, like a sexy animal attacking its prey—and swiftly flipped me over until he hovered above me. He quickly rid me of my shorts and slid my tank up before beginning to trail his hand down to the needy space between my thighs. He found me wet—no surprise there —and wasted no time before diving in with two fingers. My hips jerked in response at the way he expertly stretched me. His hands were huge, and with the way he worked me over, I assumed this was more than likely his way of preparing me for another massive appendage.

He wasn't gentle in any way, but I didn't care in the least. I was so turned on that he could've done whatever the hell he wanted to and I would've let him. This was something straight out of a porn film. I shamelessly rubbed myself against his hand while on the cusp of hyperventilating. Foster suddenly slid a third finger inside, and I gasped, consumed with how incredibly full I felt. As soon as he had me on the verge of exploding, he abruptly stopped and stood to strip out of his clothes. I continued to lay there, panting in nothing but a tank top pushed up to my neck while waiting on his next move.

I looked him up and down but stopped when I got to his throbbing erection. I figured he was big, but *holy shit.* I licked my lips, an uncontrollable need to taste him taking over me. That was exactly what I'd planned to do when he approached me again—this time, completely fucking naked—but it seemed he had a better idea. Just as I reached out to take him, he surprised me by flipping me around until he had my head hanging off the end of the sofa and my ass slightly raised against the back of it. He lowered himself to the floor, kneeling and thrust into my mouth.

I gagged, but that did nothing to deter me. I grabbed onto Foster's ass with both hands and urged him on—for my benefit as well as his. Foster took the hint and started up a harsh rhythm. It seemed he'd decided to own my mouth…*and* my throat. Anytime I gagged, it spurred him on more. I was so turned on that when he reached over to stroke my clit, I nearly combusted. I didn't think I'd ever been this worked up before, and if this was how it would be every time with him, I never wanted any other man to attempt to turn me on again.

Foster tensed, and I knew he was close. It became my mission to bring him to his knees—metaphorically speaking, considering he was quite literally already *on* his knees. So, I slid one hand from his ass to his hip, down the outside of his thigh, and teased him a bit with my nails over the sensitive skin. When he began to hold himself in the back of my throat for a little longer on his inward thrust, I slipped my hand between his legs, near my head, and massaged his balls.

He moaned my name just before he shifted, bending over at the waist. At first, I thought it was to give me more room to fondle him, but then his heated breath blasted the part of me that begged for his attention. The instant the humid air hit my arousal, I hummed around his cock, driving him even crazier. But that moment didn't last. Before I could reconcile my brain with what he was doing, his mouth came down hard on my clit, and my orgasm immediately took over. His thick shaft muffled my scream, though I was sure he enjoyed the way my throat expanded, as well as the vibrations that rippled through his pulsating erection. It was hands-down the best orgasm of my life.

Foster rolled his hips in one last, powerful thrust, and then stilled. My entire body flushed when his seed shot down the back of my throat, completing the euphoria that settled over me.

He pulled out and lowered himself to the floor above me—or was it in front of me? I was upside down after all. He sat on his haunches, steadying himself with his hands on his thighs and sighed. A small pang of guilt ricocheted in my chest for his fiancée, but that was quickly erased when the cheating bastard smiled at me.

"My body's numb...and I can't lift my head," I mumbled lethargically.

A huff of laugher rushed past his perfect lips. "That was the hottest thing I've ever experienced."

The early onset of flushed cheeks struck, so to keep him from noticing, I said, "I need help up; I can't move."

We both laughed at my predicament as he assisted me into a seated position on the couch. The humor faded, and his easy expression vanished, but before I could read too much into it, he took my head in his hands and covered my lips with his.

I didn't know what it was about him that turned me into a desperate teen, but just the feel of his mouth on mine made me want to find a tree, *any tree*, and carve, "Foster = amazing kisser," into the bark so it would live for eternity. I literally forgot my name when his tongue danced with mine.

He started slow, which was not like him at all, but the moment my arms wrapped around his neck, he immediately devoured me. Foster pulled me off the sofa and into his lap as we began to explore each other's bodies. He finished taking off my top, leaving me completely bare and palmed my breast with one hand while squeezing my ass with the other. As much as I wanted to lie back and let him have his way with me, my desire to touch him won out. My fingertips traced the lines of his defined muscles from his shoulder to his waist, and when I paused to toy with the trail of dark, coarse hair that ran from his navel to his nether regions, he groaned, "Just fucking grab it, Kam." There was no way I could've denied him anything when he commanded in such a rough, gritty tone.

Doing as I was told, I wrapped my hand around his cock and squeezed. Hard. His throaty moan insinuated that he liked it a little rough, too. So, I pumped him in my fist a few times, tightening my grip as I neared the head and twisting my hold when I reached the base. I was good at a lot of things, but no one gave a better hand job than Handy Kami. He all but agreed when he broke the kiss and held his forehead to mine, panting against my face while he uttered, "Keep this up, and I won't last long enough to get inside that sweet cunt of yours."

I relaxed my grip and slowed my ministrations—it was the best I could do; asking me to release him altogether was an asinine request. Taking the reprieve I offered, he reached over to the discarded jeans on the floor beside him and pulled out a condom from the pocket. A small part of me begged to comment on his expectations for tonight, but honestly, I was far too impatient for him to roll it on and finish me off. Luckily, Foster knew what he was doing because, in a few swift moves, he had his massive cock sheathed in latex, ready to go.

I held on to his shoulders and used his body as leverage to position myself above him, but he had other plans. As soon as I lifted my ass to line him up, he flipped me over onto my hands and knees. I didn't have time to steady myself before he grabbed my hips and promptly impaled me. Everything happened so fast. He didn't give me a chance to savor the feeling of having him seated inside me, balls deep, or even a second to etch this moment into my memory, to call upon during lonely nights or boring commercial breaks. The instant he was in, he began to move. Apparently, he didn't think

I needed to acclimate to his size before he assaulted my pussy. Granted, I *didn't* need to, but that wasn't the point. At this rate, it'd be over before I could say, "I've dreamed about this since I was seventeen." And I never wanted it to end. *Ever.*

Leaning forward so his lower abdomen melded with the base of my spine, he slid one hand from my hip down the natural line of my pelvic bone until he reached the spot I needed him the most. And as if any doubt still lingered in my mind at how experienced he was, he located the throbbing bundle of nerves on his first try. Seriously, most men could learn a few things from Foster Montgomery. Using his fingertips, he rubbed circles over my clit until my entire body was on fire. The bomb located low in my abdomen was on the verge of detonating, and I became desperate for the orgasm he was in the midst of bringing to life.

But again…Foster had another plan.

Damn him and his fucking ideas.

Here's an idea for you, buddy…make me come like an armless virgin!

As soon as he had me on the edge of ecstasy, ready to take the plunge off Orgasm Falls into Bliss Sea, he pulled away his fingers. *Fucker.* However, he didn't give me a chance to complain. He immediately hugged my midsection, pressing his slick chest flush against my back, and straightened his posture. The move lifted me off my hands until we both were in a seated position, him behind me, me in his lap, his arm wound firmly around my waist. This was new for me, and at his first upward thrust, it instantly became my new favorite.

I was lost in the sensations he smothered me with when he brought his free hand up my arm, over my chest, and wrapped his fingers around my throat. I hadn't paid him any mind until he gently squeezed my neck, somewhat cutting off of my air supply. At first, I froze, having never experienced this before. But then he forced my head back onto his shoulder and whispered into my ear, "Relax, Kam. Loosen up."

I'd heard those words before when we were kids. He'd throw insults at me, and the second I'd ball my hands into fists and glared at him, face red with anger, he'd say, *"Relax, Kami; I'm only messing with you. Geez, you should really learn to loosen up a bit."* Granted, he wasn't balls-deep in me back then, but that was neither here nor there. The point was…he'd said that to me before.

"Where'd you go, Kam?" His gravelly voice raked over my shoulder, causing my every nerve-ending to misfire. On the verge of combusting, I no longer cared what he'd said to me in our youth, just as long as he continued what he was doing to me now.

I relaxed into him while he resumed his intense, harsh thrusts. He released his hold from around my waist, though he didn't let go. Instead, he brought one hand from my hip to my breast and found my beaded nipple with his thumb and forefinger. My spine arched, my head remaining on his shoulder.

He lightly clamped my ear between his teeth, his sweltering exhales fanning against my cheek. While he repeatedly slammed into me with fervor, impatient and needy, his fingers and mouth remained gentle, calm. It was almost like he didn't know whether he wanted to fuck me or make love.

His tongue flicked my earlobe while his frantic breathing became a melody I wanted to record and play over and over again. "God, I've thought about doing this to you for as long as I can remember," he panted into my ear while ever-so-slightly tightening his grip around my neck. "You've been my wet dream for most of my life."

His words in my ear, the sensation of his hand around my throat, and his fingers pinching my nipples had me exploding. The fire he'd carefully stoked to life ignited into a raging inferno, threatening to leave me in a pile of ash and rubble.

"Oh…*fuck.*" I could barely speak past his constraint around my neck and the intense orgasm that ripped through me. It was hard enough to string two words together, much less have the capacity to utter them aloud. "Fuck" was about all I could manage at that moment.

I rarely had multiple orgasms in a day, never mind two that were that intense. By the time it finished rolling through me, leaving me with aftershocks of sheer bliss, I was spent...and he was not. I just needed to catch my breath, and then I'd be ready to keep this train going—All. Night. Long.

He dropped his hand from my neck and only loosely held me against him. Although, the momentum of his forceful thrusts—combined with my muscles that had turned to jelly—left me unable to stay upright. I fell forward, landing on my hands while he continued to plunge into me.

He gave me approximately two seconds to regroup before he grabbed my hair, tilting my head up and to the side so that he was in my peripheral vision. "I've spent all day dying to hear you call out my name while you come on my cock. Ever since your shower earlier. I *need* to hear you scream *my* name, Kam. *Mine.*" He punctuated his plea with a hearty slap across my ass.

I cried out from the sudden jolt of pleasure. Holy shit, that was unexpected. I knew from the last time that I liked it a little more than I should, but this had taken it to a whole new level of enjoyment. I panted, praying he'd do it again. And just as his warm palm finished soothing the sting his hand had left behind, he flicked his wrist and slapped me once more—in the same spot he'd delivered the last one. My eyes slammed shut as a third orgasm blindsided me. I arched my spine, lifting my ass like a cat in heat, and cried out, "*Fuck,* Foster. Ohmygod. *Oh*...Foster!"

His movements sped up, becoming frantic and jerky

right before he slammed into me one last time. His animalistic growl resounded in the room as he came hard inside me. As if we had choreographed it, we both fell to the floor in a heap of panting breaths and racing hearts.

"So much better than I thought it'd be," he whispered while tucking a strand of hair behind my ear.

I rolled my eyes. "You don't have to lie to me, Foster."

"Why do you think I'm lying?"

"Saying that you've wanted me for so long or how you thought about me all the time when we were younger is one thing while we're in the heat of the moment. But it's over now, so there's no point in saying it."

His dimple became more prominent when his lips spread into an incredible smile. "Technically, there's no point in saying it in the moment, either. Usually, those types of things are mentioned *before* the act. You know… to seal the deal. Kam, the deal has *been* sealed, so if I'm telling you that now, I'd say there's a good chance it's not to stroke your ego."

"Whatever." I sounded like a petulant teenager, but I didn't care. I waved him off with half my face pressed into the rug. I wasn't looking to get into it with him right now, not after what we just did. Drudging up the past would be better served when I hung him out to dry with his fiancée.

"Yeah, that's what I thought. Drop the subject

because you know I'm right." He pinched my ass and pushed himself off the floor. With his softened dick in his hand—holy shit, even his limp dick was bigger than most I'd seen—he asked, "Where can I dispose of this?"

Without getting up, I lifted a finger and pointed to the ceiling. "My bathroom." The last thing I needed was for Charlie to find it and ask what it was. I did *not* want to have that conversation with her just yet. "Upstairs. Last door on the right."

As much as I didn't want to put my clothes back on, I knew I needed to. If not, there was a good chance we'd fuck like rabbits until Charlie came home from school tomorrow. And while that thought was appealing, it wasn't practical. I'd been hired to keep tabs on him—he was supposed to be my *job* for crying out loud. And yes, I knew exactly where he was and what he was doing while he plowed into me, but that probably wouldn't go over too well with the Better Business Bureau.

"Well, I keep tabs on my subjects by spreading my legs; it's a very efficient strategy." I laughed at myself while I stepped into my cotton shorts and slipped my tank over my head.

When he came back downstairs, I was already dressed and back on the sofa, halfway paying attention to the movie we had started. And while my eyes were set on the TV in front of me, I watched him get dressed in the unfocused outer edges of my vision. Once he had his jeans and Henley back on, he silently slipped around the couch and awkwardly kissed me on the forehead on his way out of the room.

My mouth fell open as I stared after him, wondering what the hell had just happened. From what I could tell, he'd gone from mouth-fucking to forehead-kissing in thirty minutes. It was like high school all over again—the only difference was, he wasn't on his way to Suzie's house. Although going home to his fiancée wasn't any better.

By the time he waltzed back in, I was fuming mad. That was until he handed me a glass of water and sat next to me on the sofa. He set his glass on the table beside him; all the while, I couldn't utter a single word. Confused didn't begin to cover my mental state at the moment.

We finished watching the movie, snuggled up together like a "normal couple." Yes, I was fully aware we were definitely *not* a couple, though that hadn't stopped me from pretending for a couple of hours. We'd just fucked, and he had a fiancée—a freaking *fiancée* who'd hired me to find out if her suspicions of him cheating were warranted.

God, I'm a horrible person.

I was totally going to hell for this one. Even though Foster deserved to be taken down, his reputation ruined, Marissa didn't. She was the innocent victim in all this. And I'd just become a guilty party—hell, I'd knowingly *put* myself in that role.

When the movie was over, I'd taken the glasses of water and an empty popcorn bowl to the kitchen, and on my way back, the chime of his phone rang out. Standing behind him, I watched as he pulled his cell out of his pocket and ignored it, pressing the button on the side before slipping it back in. My stomach twisted at the reality that it had likely been Marissa.

It seemed that whenever his phone went off, his demeanor would change, and this time was no different. His shoulders slumped, and he dropped his head forward slightly, becoming a completely different person than the strong, confident alpha who'd owned my body with his an hour ago. What was even odder was when he turned around and noticed me standing there, he smiled like I'd hung the moon. It didn't seem like he was closing himself off from me at all.

I had to shake off that thought. He was a guilty, cheating bastard, capable of wearing multiple masks depending on who he was with at the moment. If not, then he wouldn't have gotten away with his games for this long. He was more than likely pissed off at whoever had called him—the woman he'd taken for a fool.

"Who was that?" I asked and pointed to his pocket. I shouldn't have asked, but I was too curious to stop myself.

He shook his head, his grin falling from his lips. "No one important."

We both stood there for a moment, trapped in a

vacuum of awkward silence. But when I held out my hand, Foster didn't hesitate to take it. The war that he battled was written all over his face, and I was torn between wanting to make it better and mentally rejoicing over his impending downfall.

With our fingers laced together, I walked him to the door. Ever since the call he had ignored, things were strained between us, though that didn't stop him from giving me a sweet yet passionate kiss in the doorway. He reluctantly pulled his lips from mine and stepped back, still holding my hand.

I ran my thumb along his cheek and asked, "What's wrong? You seem upset."

He smiled, though it didn't reach his eyes. "Nothing. I just have a lot on my mind—dealing with some personal shit, and it seems like it keeps coming back to bite me in the ass. Nothing you need to worry about; I'm taking care of it."

"That doesn't sound like nothing to me."

He shrugged. "Sometimes it gets the best of me, and I really shouldn't let it."

Figuring I wouldn't get him to confess tonight, I smiled and gave his hand a little squeeze. I wasn't sure how to say goodbye—every option I came up with felt weird. So, I lifted myself onto my tiptoes and kissed his cheek. And to make this situation even worse, I patted him on his chest. Finally, I decided that my initial idea of squeezing his hand worked better…so I did that again.

However, he refused to let me pull away, and instead, lowered his mouth closer to my ear. "I love the new grooming job. It looks good on you, Poodle," he whispered and then pulled away with a mischievous glint in his eyes.

Even without a mirror, I knew my face had turned beet red, though he eased the embarrassment with bright eyes and a goofy grin. Leave it to Foster to break the awkward, somber moment by making me laugh.

FIVE

I WOKE WEDNESDAY MORNING, feeling more refreshed than normal. Then again, I guess that was what happened when I skipped dishes and a shower and went straight to bed. Hell, I was probably asleep before Charlie, but I wasn't complaining. I rubbed my eyes and grabbed my phone, noticing I had a few missed texts. The first one came in last night after I'd fallen asleep; it was from Dana.

> Dana: Hey girl, don't forget about our
> date with Malibu and dancing tonight. I
> miss your face

God, I loved her. She knew how horrible my memory was, and although we had a standing date on Wednesdays, she knew there was a really good chance I would have forgotten had she not texted me. And that chance was amplified now, considering my mind had been too cluttered with thoughts of her brother to even remember my weekly date with her. Yes, I know…I was a terrible human being.

I exited that conversation and moved on to the next, seeing as she wouldn't be up quite yet, and I didn't want to wake her. My heartbeat stumbled when I noticed it was from Foster. I was a little surprised—and a lot elated—to hear from him. Okay, fine…I was *a lot* surprised. He hadn't so much as said one word to me since walking out of my house Monday night, and he hadn't been at Joyce's with the rest of his crew…not that I had paid any attention or anything.

> Foster: Good morning, Poodle, I hope
> you have a great day and don't enjoy
> your date too much ;)

Receiving that text had me remembering our roll on the couch—and romp on the living room floor—in *vivid* detail. Just the thought of the way he had worked me over with his fingers, then his tongue, then his dick had me squeezing my thighs together to relieve the ache. Oh, who the hell was I kidding? That ache had become a permanent fixture between my legs ever since I saw him at the gym. It didn't matter how many showers I took, how many wet dreams I had, or even how many times my fingers drifted south—all on their own, I might add—the throbbing never went away.

That boy did things to me.

And I willingly let him.

The third text was from Marissa. Nothing like hearing from Foster's fiancée to calm my overactive libido and make me realize I'd gotten *way* off track. Seeing her name was the bucket of cold water in my face that I needed to get my shit together.

> Marissa: Good Morning. Sorry to bother you so early. I was just checking in to see if you had made any headway with my case. I hope to hear from you soon.

I groaned and rolled out of bed to get Charlie off to school without responding to any of their messages.

Thank God for Starbucks. Charlie and I hit up their drive-thru window, and I got the caffeine my brain desperately needed. It didn't matter how many hours of sleep I got; I couldn't survive a day without coffee. I'd be the person who'd require a gallon of the stuff after waking from a decade-long coma. And just because I could, I stopped for a second time to get a refill on my way home after dropping off Charlie. Considering I hadn't done shit for the last two days—if you didn't count Monday's activities—I needed the added pick-me-up if I planned to get caught up with my case files.

I pulled into the driveway, surprised to find Todd's car there. I thought he was *taking a day for himself*—his words, not mine.

Inside, I found him at his desk. "Hey, I thought you were taking a *me day*?"

He looked up at me with a huge smile. "Holy shit, girl. I got the best dirt today for the Schiller's case, that cheating whore is going down." Todd's pride and joy had always been finding the cheaters; his mom had cheated on his dad, so it was his life's mission. "Last night, I was at The Cat's Meow, which you should totally check out. I found that hussy grinding all up on some young guy. Anyway, long story short, I blew off the hottie I was ready to take home and followed her. They went back to the guy's house and banged right up against the window. I mean, could she have made it any easier?"

"That's awesome. So, I get the pleasure of hanging with you today?" I pretended to sound put out, but in reality, I loved spending my days with him.

"I'm just about finished with this report. Once I'm done, I'm all yours." He made an over-the-top kissing noise, and I rolled my eyes.

"I have about some catch-up work to do, and then we can take an *us day* together."

"Sounds good to me."

We managed to get our work done, and then rewarded ourselves with a much-needed break. I grabbed my phone and responded to the texts I'd woken up to while Todd made drinks. Dana was first, obviously. I confirmed we were still on for drinks and dancing at Shenanigans, added a few wine emojis, followed by one of a girl in a red dress doing the tango, and then moved down the list of messages. Foster was next.

I kept it short, with "I'll try," I figured that was best and left it at that.

Then onto Marissa.

> Me: Good Morning, sorry for the delay, I've been really swamped lately. I should have another report for you by Monday.

> Marissa: I bet you have. Not a problem, I look forward to hearing from you.

> Me: Have a great day

We spent the afternoon lounging by the pool, drinking beverages before Todd took off to let me get ready for my girls' night.

Charlie was at her dad's, so I decided to have cereal for dinner before getting dressed for my "date" with Dana. I didn't look like a total bag of shit on a regular basis, but I definitely had the yoga pants and messy bun down to an exact science. So, I took my time with a little more makeup than usual, adding some curls to my hair, and tried on a few outfits before deciding on the final one.

The Uber driver dropped me off at the bar. When I walked in, I spotted Dana immediately—she was a curvy, beautiful redhead who literally lit up the room with her smile. I ran to her like I hadn't seen her in years, although it'd really only been a week. Dana lived an hour or so away, and with our schedules being so busy all the time, we carved out one day a week to see each— usually at Shenanigans, as it was our favorite spot. We'd spend a couple of hours chatting and talking about life, the stuff that we hadn't already talked about via text or Snapchat all week.

For the next hour, we fed the jukebox money, picking our favorite songs—same ones we chose every week— drank a few Malibu and cranberry cocktails, and danced our asses off. Between songs, or while we waited for the shooter girls to bring another round of drinks, we talked. Nothing important, basically light chatter about the guys who tried too hard to hit on us or the things we'd do to the hot bartender if only he weren't wearing a wedding band. And then we'd return to the dance floor to start the cycle all over again.

At the start of some ungodly awful song, Dana excused herself to the ladies' room—that was a very generous word for the poor excuse of a bathroom at this fine establishment. Usually, we followed the buddy system, but I was thirsty and didn't have to pee just yet. So, I headed over to the bar for a couple more cocktails and waters. As I waited for the bartender—not the hot one—to finish mixing our drinks, I happened to glance over and see a familiar face. Foster was literally two feet away from me. He turned my way, and our eyes met. I smiled and then opened my mouth to say something, but he just walked away like he didn't even know me.

What the ever-loving fuck was that?

I swear, it was fucking high school all over again.

Fuck that guy. I was about to give him a piece of my redheaded crazy when the bartender set two mixed drinks and two bottles of water in front of me. I decided to ignore Foster the way he'd ignored me, not wanting to give him the satisfaction. Instead of chewing his ass out, I sauntered by and winked at one of his friends. That was all the time I'd waste on him and spent the rest of the night focusing on the fun I was having with his sister.

And just like every week, we were closing down the bar. They had announced the last call, so while Dana got us our final round, I headed to the restroom. I only needed to touch up my lip-gloss, so I wasn't in there long, and when I walked out, I slammed right into the chest of none other than Foster fucking Montgomery. He steadied me for a moment, and then without a word, crashed his intoxicating lips to mine. I lost all common sense and kissed him back. Anyone could've come around the corner and seen us, but I couldn't care less. Then, as soon as I was ready to let him take me right then and there on the floor in front of the ladies' room, Foster pulled away. He looked me in the eyes and then walked off—*still* without saying a word.

I stood there in complete and utter shock until I

finally snapped out of it. Anger coursed through me as I walked out of the hallway, ready to rip him a new asshole. The only reason I didn't was that I spotted Foster hugging Dana goodbye. And without so much as a second glance my way, he left the bar. *Motherfucker!*

The last round of Malibu and cranberry didn't last long. I chugged that shit like it was water in the hopes it would lessen the anger rolling through me. Luckily, Dana had me laughing before she could even pick up on my disposition. We danced until the music stopped, and then we strolled outside—always the last two people in Shenanigans.

The Uber driver took us back to my place, where we collapsed onto the couch. The very last thought that went through my mind was how amazing Foster's lips felt, and how I wanted just one more taste of them before I turned him in to his fiancée.

SIX

A HARSH BANGING sound woke me from my erotic dream of Foster's tongue. I opened my eyes, trying to get a grip on what was real and what wasn't, and I saw Dana slide off the loveseat, still half-asleep. I groaned and prayed I hadn't said her brother's name in my sleep. I wasn't sure how I'd be able to explain that. It wasn't like Dana talked about him, and as far as she knew, I hadn't seen him at the bar last night.

But before my paranoia could get out of control, she mumbled, "Who the hell is knocking on your door so early in the morning?"

I glanced at the clock on the cable box beneath the TV, noting it was nearly eleven. Ignoring her question—and the time—I sat up, fully intending to answer the door. However, when I finally got to my feet, I realized Dana had taken it upon herself to greet my visitor—and knowing her, she'd give them a tongue lashing. Needing to save whoever it was from the wrath of my best friend, I quickly raced down the hall to catch up to her. But when I came around the corner and saw who stood in the doorway, I stopped short.

It was Foster. At my house. Standing in front of Dana. My best friend. His sister. His mouth hung open in shock; he definitely hadn't expected to see her there, but he quickly recovered. "Oh, good. You're awake."

"Kinda hard to sleep when someone's pounding on the door. Speaking of which…why were you beating down Kam's front door?"

He opened and closed his mouth a couple of times before saying, "I came to see you. Why else would I be here?"

"How'd you know where I was?"

"Uh…you told me last night. You don't remember? Were you really that drunk?" Judgment crossed his eyes, which was enough for Dana to drop the inquisition. "You promised me lunch."

"Now I know you're lying. I'd never offer to buy your food."

Foster relaxed with the laughter that rumbled through his chest. "No. You promised to *have* lunch with me."

"Lunch? Seriously? What happened to breakfast?"

His smirk did something to me and left me clenching my thighs together while I cowered in the hallway. "Looks like you slept through breakfast, sis. Would calling it *brunch* make you feel better?"

"It'll certainly make me feel richer, that's for sure."

"Call it whatever you want, just hurry up because I'm hungry. My treat."

"Well, in that case...let me get dressed." And then she slammed the door in his face. A second later, she opened it again. "It seems I'm already dressed."

Foster's gaze lifted from Dana's face and settled on me behind her. "Hey, Kam. Long time no see. Care to join us for lunch? Looks like a greasy burger might do you some good, too."

I rolled my eyes and bit back the anger that fought to be unleashed. "No, but thank you for the invite. I should get some notes typed up for work anyway. You two go have fun, catch up."

"Oh, you have to work? What do you do?"

"Catch bastards cheating on their significant others."

Oddly enough, he tipped his chin and nodded once. "Sounds fun. You can't make those notes later?"

"No. I have to get it done before we head out for the afternoon."

Dana looked between us a few times, probably picking up on the strange interaction. Luckily, she didn't question us. "Listen...as fun as this is to stand here and listen to the two of you fuckers catch up, I'm starving. Go wait in your car while I brush my teeth. I'll be out in a sec."

I couldn't help but laugh when she closed the door, not waiting for Foster to respond. Dana was like me— not a morning person. So she shuffled past me and went to the half-bath in the front hallway, where she kept her toiletries and brushed her teeth.

My phone chimed with an incoming text, so I went to my desk to grab it off the charger. Seeing Foster's name had me glancing over my shoulder, paranoid that Dana could somehow read it from the powder room.

> Foster: Just come and eat with us. I want to see you. I was coming over to talk, but clearly, I didn't know my sister would be here, so I had to come up with something. I don't want to intrude on your day, so we can be quick, but please just come with us.

As tempting as that would've been, I chose to ignore him—the same way he'd ignored me at the bar the night before.

"You sure you don't want to come?" Dana asked on her way to the front door, startling me. I quickly locked my phone screen, hoping she didn't notice my odd behavior.

I sat down in front of my computer to look busy. "Yeah. You go have fun with your brother."

She knew we hadn't gotten along in high school, though not the reason why, so she didn't question it. "Suit yourself. I'll bring you back whatever I don't eat. Maybe I can convince Foster I'm super hungry and order two meals and bring you home the other. Since he's paying for it and all…"

I shook my head and laughed beneath my breath. "Have fun!"

"See you soon," she practically sang as she left the house.

FOSTER DROPPED Dana off less than an hour later. Thankfully, he didn't come in—just let her out in my driveway and then left. Maybe Todd's car out front had deterred him. Either way, it didn't matter. Because Dana was back, Todd was here, and we had plans to lounge out on the beach all day. Well, for the next three hours, at least.

"It's about time, Dana," Todd grumbled next to the front door as she came downstairs in her bathing suit. He had his towel folded under his arm, ready to go. "You're taking away precious time that could be well spent ogling men at the beach."

Dana waved him off and slipped on her sandals. "You ogle men everywhere you go, so don't make it sound like I'm keeping you from anything." She wasn't lying; Todd was a bit of a manwhore and could use grocery shopping as an excuse to check out the hotties.

I couldn't complain, though...he was the best to go trolling with. He could pick out the straight men for me without even talking to them.

"Whatever, let's go." Todd opened the door and led

the way to his car. Anytime we went anywhere together, he drove. I never complained because it was better than dealing with his erratic backseat-driver tendencies. For real...if he could install a gas pedal and brake on the passenger side of my car, he would.

After finding a parking space and getting our chairs out of the trunk, I was so focused on making it down the wooden stairs to pay any attention to the people gathered in groups along the surf. I had one foot hovering over the hot sand, ready to take my first step onto the beach when I heard someone call out, *"Poodle."* Thankfully, I hadn't let go of the handrail yet and managed to catch myself before I fell on my face in front of everyone. I righted myself and quickly scanned the beachgoers in front of me. I must've been hearing things because I didn't see Foster anywhere.

"Over there." Dana pointed to a group off to the side, and I followed her line of sight, thinking she was already eyeing the beach candy. She was not.

Fuck. Fuck. Fuck.

Foster stood along the surf with his feet in the water...shirtless and staring right at me. Dana trotted over to him like she hadn't seen him in weeks. I, on the other hand, was in the midst of having a complete meltdown inside.

"Everything okay?" Todd could always read me like a book. He also tended to be a little behind the times, always the last one to grasp the obvious where everything else was concerned.

I plastered on a fake-ass smile and nodded. "If you don't count the fact that our subject is here, I'm peachy."

He blinked slowly, but when he glanced up and noticed Foster, understanding registered on his face. "I'm not sure what the big deal is, though. I mean, haven't you been seeing him anyway? Why is this any different."

"I haven't seen him since Monday night."

Todd was about to say something else when Foster called out, "Hey, Poodle." The smug bastard headed my way until we met in the middle. "You missed a good lunch."

Todd's eyebrow raised in question, but I shoved my towel at him to keep the other two from noticing and went about setting up shop in the sand. Foster tried several times to catch my attention without being obvious, which was why I avoided eye contact at all costs.

Although I tried to put up all my defenses, I decided I needed to play this from another angle. I loved being a redhead—I hated the fair complexion that came with it. I'd be a lobster within ten minutes without protection, so burnt even a light breeze along my skin would be painful. So I made sure to use plenty of sunblock, and of course, used it as a way to torture Foster. Just because I didn't look at him didn't mean I wasn't fully aware of where his attention was. And I had no doubt it was on me the entire time I lathered myself in the coconut-scented lotion. The small victory made me feel better.

Lounging in the sun wasn't my preferred pastime. To be completely honest, I hated the feeling of sand between my toes, but Dana loved everything about the beach, so I sucked it up to spend time with her. We all lazed about just people watching—which was my favorite thing to do at the beach. Actually, it was the best thing to do, no matter where I was. Nothing beat the entertainment that came along with making up stories for all the people we saw, and Foster had some good ones. Too bad I hated him and refused to let him see me laugh at his jokes.

Luckily, Todd always chimed in after Foster, which gave me an excuse to smile and allow them to believe it was at Todd's humor. He pointed to a woman in a thong bikini. The suit was cute, and she had a rockin' body, but she'd decided to work out in the middle of everyone—including children. Bent over with her ass straight up in the air, as if we all wanted a front-row seat to her goods. Some people have no shame. Everyone around us snickered and whispered, some even pointing. There was no way she couldn't hear or see it. Either she truly didn't care what others said about her, or she wanted the attention—most likely the latter.

"I can't take it anymore." I turned to Dana and shook my head. "I'm going for a swim…wanna join?" I was so hot that I felt like my skin was going to melt off.

"Nah, I'm gonna attempt to get a tan and pray I don't

burn." She rolled over and adjusted her hat. I was about to give her a guilt trip until she caved, but then Foster piped in, shutting me up.

"I'd love to go for a swim, Kam."

Dick. I gave him a *go-fuck-yourself* smile and looked at Todd, pleading for him to join us. And thank fuck he got the hint. If I had to get in the water with only Foster, I'd likely fake getting caught in a riptide just to get away from him, which would only piss me off more because then I'd have to get my hair wet.

"So…how was girls' night, Kam?" Todd tried to make small talk—he wasn't very good at it when he had to be. This man sucked at being subtle.

"It was great. Some asshole almost ruined it for us, but I just ignored him and got wasted. There were some hotties out last night, though; you should've been there." I chanced a glance a Foster. He wasn't looking at us, but I could tell he was tense by his posture.

"Umm, bitch…I wasn't invited." He laughed because he was always invited, yet he rarely came. For one reason or another, he was always busy.

I shoved him in his arm playfully, although it was pointless because he didn't budge. "Whatever. You were probably out with Peter. Or is it Ronald? Maybe Jason? I can't keep up with all your men. I'm sure you were balls deep in one of them last night. How was it?" I loved to tease him, mostly because he wasn't as slutty as I tried to make him sound.

He rolled his eyes and pushed me, just as I'd done to him moments earlier. Unfortunately for me, I did more than budge. I went flying…right in front of Foster, who tripped over me. We both landed in the surf, me on my back and him on top of me. For a moment—which felt more like an hour—we were trapped in the other's gaze, the whole world falling away and leaving only the two of us tangled up in each other.

"Oops. Did I do that?" Todd's fit of hysterical laughter broke us from the magnetic pull we'd been under. "Sorry, Foster. I didn't mean to get you in the crossfire."

Foster pulled himself up first and then reached for me, but I brushed him off. He'd touched me enough for the day—at least, that's what I had to tell myself to keep from grabbing his hand and pulling him back on top of me. That thought alone had me searching the beach for Dana, praying she hadn't witnessed the tumble in the surf. Thank God she was still sunbathing with her hat covering her face. That was certainly not something I wanted to explain to her.

I stood and kicked water at Todd. "You fucker."

Todd nearly doubled over in amusement. He had this infectious laugh when he really got going, and no matter how hard I tried, I couldn't win against the need to join in on the humor. However, it seemed Foster was more immune to it than I was, because he stood there, watching the two of us interact without even a hint of a smile on his intoxicating lips.

We finally made our way out farther until the water came to our chests—well, on me, anyway; on the guys, it was more like their waists. Being out this far gave us some sort of privacy, which I normally preferred, yet having Foster so close almost made me wish we had a throng of people around us. Although, I was sure he would've found a way to get close to me no matter what. Every time he was within arm's reach, he made sure I was aware by brushing against me or grabbing my ass under the water. Any excuse for contact, he took it.

When he wrapped his arm around my waist and held my back against his chest, using me as a human shield to protect himself from Todd's water attack, I turned my attention to the shore. I was desperate for any excuse to get away from him, and as soon as I noticed that Dana was still on her stomach, I knew I'd found the perfect one. "Oh, shit…how long have we been out here?"

Todd checked his watch, completely oblivious to everything—Foster's interest in touching me, my desire to get away from him, and my best friend asleep on the beach. "I'm not sure…an hour or so maybe? I wasn't really paying attention to the time. Why? You have a hot date tonight or something?"

"Funny, you know that rarely happens." I hadn't thought about my words until Foster cleared his throat. *Crap.*

"No, Dana's been lying like that since we left her. She's going to burn."

"Didn't she put something on when you did?" It was no surprise that Foster had to ask that, proving my theory that his eyes had been on me, and *only* me, while I coated myself in sunscreen.

"Yeah, *something*. She wanted to get a tan, so she sprayed herself with SPF fifteen while I used the fifty-plus lotion." I peered down at my shoulder and winced. "If I'm pink after practically bathing in that crap, I don't even want to think about what shade of pain she's in right now."

They both squinted toward the beach at Dana lying on her towel, and then looked at each other with a shrug. This budding bromance needed to end—STAT. It was too much to handle, so I started to wade through the water toward the shore, leaving them behind. Halfway there, they passed me by, moving much faster in the waves than I did. Though I couldn't complain because the view was nice. Foster's back muscles rippled with each step he took. By the time we made it to dry land, I was wetter than I had been while actually *in* the water—and I wasn't talking about my suit.

I didn't have to look at Dana twice to see that she was fried. While the guys just stood there, joking about how they should've used my sunscreen to draw a penis on her back before she had fallen asleep, I used my towel to wring out my hair. As soon as I had the material soaked enough to be useful, I draped it over her.

Dana yelped and practically jumped off the ground. "What the fuck? That's cold!" She didn't sound very happy, but she'd be even more pissed when she found out how burnt she was. You'd think after being blistered by the sun once that she would've learned her lesson and accepted the curse of fair skin. But no. I'd lost count of how many times she had done this, yet she continued to believe she could tan.

"I have some lotion in the car. You want to come with, Kam?" Todd's expression made it clear that I didn't have an option. He didn't often use the arbitrary stare-down on me, and it was even rarer to see the single, arched brow without it being directed at someone else. So, when he gave me both, it was enough to know that while he posed it as a question, it was more of a subtle demand.

Pushy motherfucker.

But I obliged—not because I was scared of the asshat or anything, but because it gave me an excuse to get away from Foster. And after an hour of being tortured by his hands in the ocean, it was either follow Todd to the car or risk an indecent-exposure charge for stripping down to nothing and letting Foster have his way with me. That woman and her thong were PG compared to what I would've done to Foster had Todd not dragged me away when he did.

However, we only got a few feet away before Todd started on me. "What the fuck is going on?"

I turned to him, my mouth hanging open in mock surprise. "What do you mean?"

"Cut the crap, Kam. You know that innocent shit doesn't work on me. You forget how well I can read you. So stop the act and just tell me what's going on. That man touched you every single chance he got, and as I recall, we agreed you were allowed to look with your eyes, not your hands." He stopped and crossed his arms over his bare chest. "So…tell me, why was he all over you?"

"He was *not* all over me. Don't be ridiculous." I tried to shrug it off, which never seemed to work with Todd, but this time, his attention shifted to something over my shoulder.

His mouth fell open, and it seemed like he'd stopped breathing. Clearly, he'd moved on to something far more entertaining than Foster and me. "Holy fucking shit, Kam. Isn't that Marissa?"

I turned around to see that he was right. About thirty feet away, standing in front of Foster, was Marissa. "Wait…how do you know what she looks like?" I stared at Todd questioningly.

"Seriously? I'm your business partner. I know all our cases and clients. Since she's a client, I know who she is."

"There's no way you recognized her from the crappy picture on her photocopied ID."

He sighed, seemingly exasperated with me. "It appears I'm a much better investigator than you. Have you ever heard of social media, darling? You should check it out sometime, maybe move your skillset into the new millennium. I know you're used to communicating by finger-painting on rocks in caves, but in this century, we use Facebook and Instagram." He nearly toppled over from laughter. Making fun of me amused him to no end.

"Implying that I'm from the Dark Ages won't get you anywhere, my friend."

Ignoring him, I turned back to find Marissa's hands flailing in the air like some kind of scorned mistress after discovering the truth about her lover—well shit, I guess that would've been me in this case. I couldn't make out a word that they were saying; all I could tell from the exchange was that they were definitely arguing. Dana was now on her feet, regarding Marissa with anger marring her features. Foster's posture was stiff, making him appear defensive.

After a few minutes, I heard Foster shout, *"Not that it's any of your business, but she's my fucking sister!"*

"She doesn't know, Dana? How can you be engaged to someone and not recognize their sister?" Todd was right, although there could've been a dozen plausible excuses. What he or I found odd might've been acceptable to others. After all, I was a prime example of someone who'd never gotten along with her husband's sibling, and if I'd had it my way, I would've never been in the same room as Landon's brother.

All of a sudden, I realized Marissa was heading our way. I'd been too lost in thought over her not recognizing Dana and my hatred for the man who shared my ex's face that I didn't notice she had walked away from Foster until it was almost too late.

"Todd, open your car now." It was meant to be a whisper-yell, though it basically came out in the jumbled mess of shaky, panic-filled words that even I couldn't translate.

He didn't bother trying to hide his confusion, yet he did as I asked. We both jumped into his car, and I grabbed the sides of his face, pretending to make out with him. He struggled, of course, but Marissa didn't notice, likely too pissed off at the thought of catching her fiancé with another woman to care what a couple of strangers were doing with each other in a hot car at the beach. She got into a convertible parked a little way down, and as soon as she tore out of the lot, I let him go.

"What the hell, Kam?" He wiped his mouth with the back of his hand as if our lips had actually touched. "You know you don't have the right equipment. I knew this day would come. I'm too attractive to resist." He took my hand in his and regarded me with a seriousness etched into his expression. "You are a beautiful woman, but—"

"Shut the fuck up." I yanked my hand away. "I was

trying to avoid being seen by Marissa. I doubt she'd be very happy if she found us paling around with her fiancé at the beach."

"Are you for real right now?" Rather than being understanding about my motive to fake kiss him, he acted repulsed and dumbfounded. "First of all, when she showed up, we weren't anywhere near him, so 'paling around' is a bit overboard, don't you think?"

"No, but I think *you're* a bit overboard right now."

"Secondly," he said and held up two fingers. "She parked like halfway across the lot. We could've stayed where we were, and she wouldn't have seen us. There was no need to get in this hot box of a car, let alone put your face that close to mine."

"Your dramatics are entertaining. Please, continue. Got a *thirdly* in there somewhere?" I might've succeeded at stifling my laughter, though I failed at hiding my grin.

Todd pursed his lips and glared at me. "No, but I do have a theory."

"Oh, yeah? Enlighten me, then. What's this theory you speak of?"

"You're paranoid. And you only get that way when you have something to hide, which all seems to go back to Foster getting all handsy with you in the water like he had permission to touch you intimately. Tell me, Kam… why would he think that?"

"Never mind. I no longer care about your theories. You're starting to sound like those conspiracy people who believe the government is hiding aliens in some top-secret field on U.S. soil. It's unbecoming of you." I reached for the door handle, but he stopped me with a hand on my shoulder.

"You have five seconds to tell me, or I'll go ask the man of the hour."

He was bluffing—he had to be. Asking Foster would blow the entire investigation. Although, I was pretty sure sleeping with him had already done that, but that wasn't the point. In all honesty, I'd been dying to tell *someone* about Monday night, but I worried about Todd's reaction almost as much as I feared Dana's—not that telling her was even an option. I could only imagine how that conversation would go.

Hey, Dana. So, funny story…I fucked your brother. Yeah, I know he's engaged to be married. How do I know? Because his bride-to-be hired me to find out if he was cheating. I couldn't catch him with another woman, so I decided to spread my legs and see if he'd take the bait. In case you're wondering, …he took it. Oh, and before I forget, we used to fuck around a lot back in the day. I kept that from you, too.

Yeah…no, thank you. That wouldn't go over too well.

"Fine." I huffed and fell back into the seat, though I did open the door to let out some of the heat to keep from suffocating to death. "He came over to the house Monday night to watch a movie and hang out."

Todd held up one finger to silence me, and then asked, "You mean Monday, as in three days ago?"

When I nodded, he followed his question up with, "The same night, Charlie was at her little friend's house?"

"Yes, Todd. It's all the same freaking Monday. Would you like to hear the rest?"

"I would love that. Carry on."

"Anyway, so he came over to watch a movie. We were on the couch, laughing at Seth Rogen one minute, and the next, he had me upside down on the sofa with his cock shoved down my throat, fucking my mouth like a freaking pro."

"I have so many questions...and I'm not sure where to begin."

Here it came, the lectures I wanted to avoid. I couldn't even look at him, knowing if I did, all I'd see staring back at me would be an utter disappointment. "Just get it over with, Todd."

"Okay...first of all, which Seth Rogen movie were you watching?"

His question stunned me at first, but then I figured he probably asked it to ease me into the tougher ones. *"Knocked up."*

"Hmmm..." He nodded slowly in my peripheral vision. "Is he as big as he looks?"

I could no longer *not* look at him. "Huh? Who?"

"Seth Rogen." Todd pulled his head back slightly and shook his head while giving me a *you-can't-be-that-stupid* look, curled upper lip, and pinched brow included.

"Foster, you dumb cow. Who the hell else would I be talking about?"

"Oh." I tucked my bottom lip between my teeth to ward off the blush creeping up my neck. I dragged it back out before admitting, "Huge. Like…ohmygod big. And you know how some guys who are blessed with an elephant trunk as a dick are clueless how to use it?"

He nodded.

"Well, he is *not* one of them."

"You might be giving him too much credit here. I mean, a successful blowjob is awarded more often to the giver than the receiver. I've enjoyed giving to a few who made the main attraction seem very promising, only to epically fail when…well, when push came to shove. If you get my drift."

"No, I get it, but I can tell you he's skilled in *every* aspect." I'd gotten so into the excitement of finally getting to talk to someone about the amazing sex I'd had with Foster that I totally forgot *who* I was about to tell and *how much* he wasn't supposed to know.

Todd groaned and dropped his face into his hands. "Kam. This is bad. This is so very bad."

"I know. That's why I've been avoiding him since he left that night. I had no idea he was coming today. Apparently, Dana invited him when he took her out for brunch today, and she didn't think to tell me because she didn't think it would be a big deal. I couldn't exactly tell her why it is, in fact, a big deal. It's a huge fucking deal." My anxiety was through the roof.

"Want to know what else is a big deal? The fact that you had sex with him."

I dropped my head against the back of the seat and stared at the sky through the sunroof. "Don't remind me. I already feel like shit about it, and now I have to figure out how to deal with Marissa."

"Whatever you do, you can't tell her. Got it?" He shifted to face me and waited until I made eye contact before finishing. "You got paid to do a job...I'm not entirely sure, but I believe that by taking the money and then having sex with him, you just became a prostitute."

"A what?" I wasn't sure if I wanted to laugh or scream.

"You were essentially paid for sex." When I started to argue, he put his hand in my face and added, "Again, I'm not clear on the specifics, but I think you're somewhere in the blurry line. It's best if she never finds out. In fact, just to be safe, I'll take the money on this one so you can honestly say you never received a dime."

I shoved him in the shoulder and shook my head. "Not going to happen."

"Worth a shot. But if you think this conversation is over, you're wrong." He pointed toward the beach through the windshield. "Looks like they're packing up to leave. I'll go get our towels and give Dana the lotion, but when I get back, we will finish talking about it on our way home."

"Wait…you seriously have lotion? I thought that was an excuse to ask me about Foster without either of them around."

"Don't be silly. Everyone should carry lotion with them." And with that, he got out of the car and bounded down the wooden steps while I remained in the passenger seat. I snapped out of it and followed behind him.

True to his word, when he came back, he didn't waste a second before jumping into the lecture I knew was coming. And once he felt he'd efficiently conveyed the seriousness of my situation, he hounded me for all the details. And I mean *all* of them. He truly was a sick individual, but I loved him anyway.

SEVEN

AFTER DROPPING Charlie off at school on Friday, I headed to Starbucks to meet Marissa. I'd emailed her after getting home from the beach yesterday and asked her to meet me this morning. She didn't know it, but I planned to give her back the money she'd paid when hiring me. Todd was right…I'd totally fucked this up and had allowed it to get out of hand. I was a better PI than this, and I needed to do something to make it right.

As soon as I sat down at an empty table in the back, a large hand gripped my shoulder. I instantly knew it was Foster by the way my skin heated at his touch. I had avoided him since leaving the beach—I'd parked in the garage, didn't answer the door, and ignored every text and call that had come from his number. Honestly, this didn't surprise me too much, although it couldn't have come at a worse time.

He sat down beside me, leaving no room to run, but inside, that was all I wanted to do. Marissa was supposed to be here any minute, and she couldn't find Foster there with me.

"What are you doing here?" I glanced at the front door, making sure Marissa hadn't already walked in.

"You've been avoiding me. I've called, sent texts—that I know you read—and even drove by your house a couple of times, but you weren't home. So, when I saw your car pull in here, I decided it was worth a shot. At least now, you can't ignore me. What the fuck happened, Kam?" His tone was full of hurt and confusion.

"You can't be here right now, Foster. I'm waiting for a client, and she'll be here any second. I need you to go. It would be completely unprofessional if she showed up and you were here." I was freaking the hell out, unsure if he would listen and leave like I'd asked. His body language said he wouldn't so much as get out of the chair until he got what he came for.

"Kamryn…" He ran his hand down his face as if I exhausted him—*it's the other way around, buddy.* "I'll go, but only if you tell me why you've been avoiding me." He stared into my eyes, begging me to give him an answer.

I debated; if I told him the truth, there was a chance he'd confess everything to Marissa, which in turn, could ruin my reputation as a business owner. I wouldn't survive if everyone believed I'd slept with the very people I'd been hired to investigate. On the other hand, if

I lied and gave him some equally plausible excuse, I ran the risk of him trying to make it right.

"I can't do this right now, Foster." I went with option number three—stall. "Let me get through this meeting, and then we'll talk about it. Okay?"

"Sure. I can wait."

"No!" I all but shouted. If that didn't raise a gigantic red flag, I didn't know what would. "I mean…it could be a while. I have a lot to discuss with my client. Plus, it's personal. I'm sure she doesn't want anyone to overhear."

His eyes narrowed the tiniest bit as he scanned the entire seating area of the coffee shop. "I understand that I don't run the same kind of business you do, and my conversations with clients are…well, not as personal as yours are, but I'd say if you wanted privacy to discuss sensitive information, I wouldn't recommend a public place where anyone can listen in."

"Listen…" I placed my hand over his, trying to appear far less freaked out than how I felt on the inside. "I appreciate your advice, so don't take what I'm about to say wrong. You see, there's a very big difference between that woman"—I pointed to a lady sitting two tables away—"eavesdropping during my meeting, and you sitting with us."

"I get it." He scooted his chair back and stood. The air around me became much lighter and easier to breathe… until he added, "I'll just wait in that empty seat over there."

I followed his finger to a loveseat and two chairs near the entrance. The relief I'd felt when he stood up vanished, and I was back to panic mode. "That's not what I meant, Foster. She'll notice you watching."

"In the amount of time you've wasted by arguing with me, you could've told me what I came here for. Everything was fine—or so I thought—and the next thing I know, you're making snide comments, avoiding me, not responding to my texts… what gives, Kam?"

"You seriously don't know? I doubt that." I could've very well just told him what I knew, but for some reason, the words refused to come out. Even the thought of saying, "you're engaged," made my heart threaten to quit working.

His brows knitted in confusion. "No, I don't. Honestly, Kam…I have no idea what happened. Did Monday night freak you out? You seemed fine afterward while we finished watching the movie, so I didn't think you were bothered by it. Then on Wednesday, you walked right past me and eye-fucked one of my boys as if I weren't sitting right there. So no…I'm completely lost as to why you've been ignoring me."

It seemed we had a lot more to discuss than just his relationship status. Although, throwing that out there would eliminate the need to talk about the rest. But then, I'd be back at square one without the opportunity to speak my mind about how he'd made me feel in high school, as well as over the last week. And as much as I wanted this to be over and done with, I refused to cut the cord until I had everything off my chest.

I pushed myself out of my seat and placed my palm in the center of his chest. Had I been able to think of anything other than the rejection on his face, I wouldn't have done that. But it seemed when he was around, the entire world faded away. I opened my mouth to say something, yet I wasn't given a chance to utter a single word. Because in an instant, I became very aware of my surroundings.

"Well, isn't this cute?" Marissa stood a few feet away with her arms crossed over her chest, a scowl marring her otherwise perfect features.

My hand dropped just as Foster stepped away. This was what I had hoped to avoid. Unfortunately, that didn't happen, and now, I was smack-dab in the middle of a *Jerry Springer* episode.

"Marissa..." It was unclear if Foster had meant that as a question, or if he always said her name with a lilt at the end. "What are you doing here?"

"I could ask you the same thing. I came to meet with Kamryn."

Foster glanced between the two of us, and I tried like hell to offer an apology with my eyes, though he didn't seem to understand it. "Marissa's your client? The one you're waiting on?"

"Why...does that surprise you, Foster?" Marissa took a step closer, her hatred now aimed directly at him.

"Because, I have to say, finding you two here together surprises the hell out of me."

I glanced around the room, wondering how much attention we'd garnered. None. How was it that I could have all eyes on me while eating an egg sandwich in this place, but when three people are standing up, one of which practically had horns coming out of her skull, no one even noticed?

Foster moved to stand between us, shielding me with his massive arm. I was too focused on how snug the sleeve of his T-shirt fit around his bicep to think about his motivation for standing in front of me. In the back of my mind, I assumed he'd done it to hide me as if Marissa hadn't already seen us together, let alone with my hand intimately on his chest. But had I truly given it thought, I might've questioned his protectiveness.

"I guess it's a little shocking to find out you two know each other." His voice rumbled through his chest, making it sound deeper from behind him.

"Imagine how I feel to come in here and see you two together. Have you been fucking her? Is that what this is about?"

Now, *that* had to have earned at least one person's attention. But again, as I searched the room for a set of eyes, any set of eyes, I found none. You better believe if I so much as whispered "hell" in public, there'd be someone slapping their hands over a child's ears while gasping in astonishment.

"Can we talk about this somewhere else?" he asked, almost pleading.

Oh God. My heart sank, and my stomach twisted into so many knots I was about to throw up. I needed to put an end to this before he confessed everything. Why did he have to choose *now* to grow a conscience? It would've been better had he continued with his douche ways and just lied.

"There's really no need to talk about this." I stepped to the side to address Marissa without having to peer over Foster's incredible arm. "The answer is no. We aren't sleeping together. His sister is my best friend, so he and I go way back. That's all this is. Nothing more."

"And…what? You just decided to keep that piece of information from me when I hired you? You didn't think I had a right to know?"

Foster turned to the side, facing us both with his narrowed gaze and deeply creased forehead. Absolute bewilderment painted his expression when he set his sights on his fiancée. "What does it matter if we knew each other years ago?" And when he locked me in his stare, betrayal flashed in his brown eyes. "Did you know about us when she hired you?" he asked, pointing between Marissa and himself as if I didn't know the "us" he was referring to.

I couldn't speak. Like a child getting caught doing something wrong, I simply stared at him, begging him with my eyes to understand. Although, I wasn't sure what I tried to get him to understand, considering it seemed he'd comprehended the situation well enough.

"So that's what this has been about for you? Why? I mean, I know Dana's said you didn't like me much when we were younger, but I just figured that was what you told her so she wouldn't know about us. I didn't think she was right."

He regarded me with such sadness, such pain that it seemed like I'd stabbed him in the chest, and then twisted the knife for fun. I was torn between the emotions his eyes cast on me, and the words I needed to form to make things right with him. Unfortunately, I wasn't able to come up with anything fast enough.

He blew out a rushed exhale, ran his hand through his hair, and mumbled, "Never mind," before walking away.

I was seconds away from chasing after him when I realized Marissa was still there. She hadn't followed him, hadn't budged an inch from where she stood with her arms crossed. Although now, she aimed her disgust at me.

"Listen…I know it's a little late, and you probably won't believe me, but I honestly asked you to meet me today, so I could give you back the money you paid and take myself off this case."

"You're right. I don't believe you. But I guess it doesn't matter anymore, does it? I suspected he was cheating on me. I just didn't for one second think it was with the same person I had hired to give me answers. Now it makes sense that you never caught him with anyone else. You clearly weren't going to turn yourself in, so what was your endgame here? Take my money and carry on with your affair behind my back?"

Her anger was still very much apparent, though the rest of her demeanor struck me as odd—way too calm and collected. It wasn't what I expected from a woman who'd just caught her fiancé and investigator together. I hadn't been a PI for long, only since the divorce, but in that time, I'd been the bearer of bad news on more than one occasion. And while this situation was a little different than those—despite what I'd done with Foster, I had *not* slept with anyone from my other cases—her reaction didn't fit. Or, should I say, *lack* of reaction. Then again, everyone handled their emotions differently, so I brushed it off and went back to the issue at hand.

"No, Marissa. That's not it at all. Honestly, when I got your initial email, asking me to investigate Foster, I saw it as an opportunity to get back at him for all the shit he'd put me through years ago."

An older lady at the table beside us, which had been empty when Marissa had first shown up, leaned over, and said, "The foul language isn't needed. Not everyone finds the use of expletives acceptable. Talking like trash only leads people to assume you *are* trash."

My mouth dropped open, and I was sure my eyes were twice their normal size as I stared at the woman in disbelief. I was over forty years old, for fuck's sake. But there she was, lecturing me like I was some teeny-bopper —you know the kind, the gaggle of high school kids who gather in groups outside the theater without actually watching a movie. In my day, it was the mall. Now that I think of it, online shopping has totally destroyed this country's youth by eliminating the need for malls… hordes of teens spending their parents' money not only had a huge economic advantage, but those places closed at a reasonable time, whereas a theater offered nothing but an unsupervised place for kids to get high and have sex in the back of someone's car.

Charlie would *never* go to the movies alone.

But I digress.

I blinked at the hag a few times and said, "Where were you when this one over here dropped the F-bomb?" I twisted my wrist and stuck out my thumb in Marissa's direction.

"Thankfully, not here." The woman glanced at my client with an easy expression. "Although, I doubt she would've said something so ugly. She doesn't look like the type."

I balked, fully convinced I was being set up. "And *I* do?"

She eyed me with a slightly curled top lip. "Well… you are wearing what appears to be sleepwear in public, so I'm not sure what to think."

This bitch was crazy. I looked down to make sure I

had, in fact, changed clothes this morning before leaving the house and not just dreamed that I had—hey, that had happened before—and then met her stare once more. "These are Lululemon leggings! A totally acceptable form of outerwear!"

Someone approached me from the side and cleared his throat. When I broke away from the whitehaired prude, I found a timid Starbucks's employee, green apron, and all, standing before me. "I'm sorry, ma'am, but I have to ask you to keep it down. It seems you're disrupting the atmosphere for others." He swallowed harshly, dropped his gaze to the table beside me, and added, "If you'd prefer, we offer outside seating with lovely umbrellas to block the sun."

There were many things I wanted to say to this guy, but I kept my mouth shut—mostly because he looked like a sweet person, and he didn't deserve my wrath. Instead, I smiled at him, and in the sweetest voice I could muster, I apologized. "I'm so very sorry…" I peeked at his name written in black marker on the front of his apron. "…Kevin. I never meant to ruin anyone's experience here."

He nodded and fled to his station behind the counter. Poor guy.

I glared at the old woman, yet she no longer paid me any attention. Her eyes scanned the pages of the book in her hands, and I smiled at the thought of Fabio gracing its cover. Then I brought my focus back to Marissa, who oddly enough, still stood in the same spot, in the same position, with the same, dismissive demeanor.

"I don't remember where we were." *Foster, money, motive…* "Ah, yes. I recall now."

Apparently, she didn't hear that last part and took it upon herself to get us back on track. "You were about to tell me some sob story to justify what you did with my fiancé behind my back."

"No. That's not it. Did I recognize him when I opened your email? Yes. Did I purposely leave out the fact that I knew him eons ago and have remained best friends with his sister? Again, yes. But I honestly didn't mean any harm by it. I saw a way to get back at him for how he'd treated me in the past, and I didn't think about how that deception would affect you. And for that, I'm deeply sorry."

"*For that?*" She finally dropped her arms. Granted, she balled her hands into fists and then settled them on her hips the way my mother used to do when I'd get in trouble, but at least she no longer squeezed her tits together. "You're not deeply sorry for sleeping with the man I've spent the last year planning a future with?"

I couldn't be sure without digging through our earlier conversations, but something made me think she'd told me they had only been engaged for a few months. I specifically recalled her saying something along the lines of wanting to find out now instead of wasting time planning a wedding that might not ever happen if her suspicions were right. In fact, I also remembered thinking that it was odd she would've accepted Foster's proposal if she believed he was unfaithful. But that would have to wait until I got home.

"Yes. I'm unbelievably remorseful about that. More than you know."

"You should be," the old woman beside us muttered without taking her eyes off her book.

When I returned my attention to Marissa, she just stood there, shaking her head in disappointment, like I'd promised her a lollipop and didn't deliver. Again, it was all very odd. "So you admit it?"

I was lost. "Admit what?"

"That you've been sleeping with him."

Well, shit. How the hell did I get myself in this mess? The plan was to avoid, distract, and deny. She'd foiled the avoidance, and while the prude next to me aided in my efforts to distract Marissa, it didn't prove to be very successful, and now, I'd somehow passed up the chance to deny and went straight to admitting fault.

There was no point in dragging this out. I grabbed my checkbook from my purse and tore out the pre-written refund. "I can stand here all day and tell you how none of this was my intention, and how I'd do it all differently if I could, but I won't waste your time."

She snatched the check out of my hand, though she didn't leave. Instead, she held the small piece of paper between her fingertips and scrutinized it as if verifying it wasn't fake.

"I really do hope the two of you can work this out. If it means anything, I never did catch Foster so much as talking to another woman. He either worked, went to the gym, or hung out with other guys." I didn't particularly like the idea of Foster marrying this chick, nor did I care what they decided to do about their wedding, but at this point, I needed to salvage something. And right now, I needed that *something* to be my business and reputation. Sure, it was slightly selfish, but in reality, the backlash of this wouldn't affect just me—it'd ruin Todd, as well.

Marissa folded the check and slipped it into her back pocket, a sliver of a grin curling her painted lips. "Oh, I'm way past that. You did me a favor. Now I can move on without the constant what-ifs. I feel like I've been holding onto the good parts of him, too afraid I'd miss out if I let him go, and now I don't have to worry about that anymore. So he's all yours if you still want him. If you think about it, I should be *thanking* you." She smiled without showing teeth, then added, "But I won't," before she trotted out of the coffee shop.

I watched as she disappeared through the front door, and then plopped myself into the seat I'd been in before all this started. Before Foster tracked me down and refused to leave. Before Marissa showed up and caught me touching her man. Before the old bitty next to me made me question leggings in public.

This whole day had gone to shit, and it was only ten in the morning.

My phone vibrated through my bag, which hung on the back of the wooden chair. I blindly grabbed it, holding on to the smallest hope that it would be Foster's name on the screen. I never thought I'd say it, but the fact that it wasn't him saddened me. He'd religiously texted me for the last two days, all of which I'd ignored, and now, when I wanted to hear from him the most, he chose to cut me off.

I responded to Todd's text, letting him know I'd refunded Marissa while skipping over the rest of the details. Those would have to be explained in person, although it would be nice if he just never found out about them.

After sending my text to Todd, letting him know my plans for the day, I pulled up Foster's conversation thread and read through the messages I'd ignored since Wednesday night. My chest constricted as I read his words to myself. Prior to seeing the pain in his eyes, they had come across arrogant, the way I was used to him sounding. Though now, I could clearly see the desperation before me.

> Me: I don't like the way we left things today. Once the dust settles, do you think maybe we could talk? Doesn't have to be today or even this weekend if you're not up to it. I'm sure you'll be busy dealing with everything, so I understand. I just don't want too much time to pass without the chance to explain.

It was stupid to think he'd read it. And even more stupid to think he'd actually reply. Both of which became abundantly clear as I sat there, alone in Starbucks, staring at my screen, waiting for the "read" notification to pop up beneath my text box. Finally, after what felt like a hundred years, I gave up and decided to go home. At least there, I wouldn't be judged by someone's granny.

I had my phone in my purse, my purse strap over my shoulder, and my pride in the toilet as I made my way outside. Only to discover that I wouldn't be going anywhere with four flat tires. My very first thought was, *whose dog did I kick in a past life to get this kind of luck?* Then I asked myself, *how would I have popped all four tires without noticing I'd run over anything?* But the more I stared blankly at the deflated rubber, the more I began to understand.

I hadn't kicked anyone's dog.

I'd slept with someone's fiancé.

Oh, and unfortunately, that had happened in *this* life.

EIGHT

WHILE SITTING beneath one of the *lovely* umbrellas in front of Starbucks, waiting for the tow truck to arrive, Charlie's school called. They had early dismissal today, and I hadn't picked her up. Great…just what I needed—forgetting my kid at school.

As much as I hated to do it, I called Landon to see if he'd be able to get her, at least until I could pick her up from his house. Luckily, my ex loved his daughter, so he made no qualms about leaving work early. Although, I was sure I'd feel the sting later when he threw this back in my face. Oh well. I was desperate.

The assholes at the body shop had warned me that they were behind, but that they'd get to me as fast as they could. By two o'clock, I had started to believe I'd die outside Starbucks. Even with the umbrella shading me from the sun—thank God for that, because I didn't have any sunblock with me—it was still hot as hades. If I had to wait much longer, there was a strong possibility that I'd end up stripping down to my bra, which would bring on a whole new set of issues. And for the first time since I'd freed my bearded clam, I wished I had a pair of panties…because, you know, the chances of me *actually* taking off my clothes to cool down were great.

Thankfully, the tow truck pulled up along the curb seconds before my top came off. Yeah, right; that was laughable. Charlie had done a number on the girls, and every time I'd mention having them "fixed," Landon had assured me that I didn't need it. Well, maybe *that* husband didn't mind the flapjacks on my chest, but that didn't mean the next one—if there ever were one— would feel the same.

At first, the driver refused to give me a lift to the shop. But the thought of calling someone to get me nearly pushed me over the edge. That's when the waterworks started, and as luck would have it, Barry had a weak spot for a crying woman.

Now, I just had to wait for them to replace the tires.

"Who'd you piss off?" Barry asked when he strolled into the waiting room about an hour later. "Looks like someone took out their anger on your car with a knife to all four wheels. Remind me not to get on their bad side."

I waved him off, not caring to get into the details and paraphrased. "My ex's fiancée—well, probably not anymore—doesn't seem to care much for me."

"A *woman* did that?" He hitched his thumb over his shoulder and pointed to the garage behind him. "I thought for sure it was a guy. Takes a lot of strength to really get in there the way she did. Damn."

There was a chance I'd look back on this in the future and laugh...but I didn't find it too humorous while drowning in the moment.

"Anyway," he continued, "I've got good news, and I've got bad news. We can get these babies swapped out today and send you home with four brand-new tires. Unfortunately, they aren't cheap, so—"

"Don't worry about the cost." I was a little relieved that the bad news wasn't really bad. At least something would go right today. "I wasn't prepared to spend any money on tires, but I don't really have much of an option."

"Oh...well, that's good. But what I was going to say was, with the price tag being as high as it is, we don't keep them in stock. Not too many people come in needing a full set without making an appointment first. So, we have to get them from another store."

"Okay?" I waited for him to explain what the problem was.

"The closest store is about an hour away."

Seriously, there was no way my luck had become *this* bad.

PSA: If you ever find yourself tempted to sleep with someone who's in an ongoing relationship with anyone other than *you*—don't. The amount of shit life will dump on you isn't worth it.

Although, the memory of what Foster had done to me less than a week ago made the time pass fairly quickly. Before I knew it, four hours had gone by, and I was finally able to leave the shop. Thank. God. I wasn't sure I could handle the smell of motor oil for another minute.

But just when I thought my streak of bad luck was over, I called Landon to let him know I was on my way to pick up Charlie. Apparently, they were in the middle of an intense game of Monopoly, and he thought it made sense if she stayed the night and came home in the morning. I contemplated pulling a few hairs from Charlie's head to have them tested for drugs because she had agreed with him.

Fuckers. They were all fuckers. Every last one of them starting with Marissa and ending with Landon, with a string of grease-stained mechanics in between. And considering Todd was too busy balancing his two men to stay in and drink with me tonight, and Dana was out of town for the weekend, they were both fuckers, too.

"What the…?" I slowed as I pulled up to my house, staring through the side window while creeping toward the driveway. "That dirty chode sucking fuckwit! I'll strangle that little cuntflap until her tiny pecker-head pops off!" I screamed while beating my fist against my steering wheel.

I pressed on the gas pedal a little harder than intended and whipped into my driveway, giving me a front-row view of the new paint job my house had undergone while I waited on fancy fucking tires that had to be imported. Hot-pink sentiments stretched along the front of my custom painted garage, letting everyone who drove by know how much of a whore I was...in very colorful verbiage.

"Oh, this jizz puddle messed with the wrong bitch," I mumbled to myself as I slid out of the car. "Just you wait, you crazy-ass dickbag. Wait until I get my hands on you. You'll regret the day your cock lovin' mama brought your cum-dumpster ass into this world." I took a breath and calmed down. That was wrong of me...I had no idea if Marissa's mom liked dick—for all I knew, she was in a very healthy relationship with a really nice woman.

I offered up a silent apology for my possibly misguided assumption.

Although, it wasn't that farfetched. I mean, her daughter *had* turned out to be quite the infected snatch. Then again, in the off-chance Charlie grew up to be less than stellar, I'd hate it if someone cursed my name. And with the way my luck was going, the odds were against me. So, it was best to keep this twatwaffle's mom out of it.

I reached over the driver's seat and grabbed my cell out of the cupholder. After a few taps, I had her number pulled up and the line connecting. Only to hit a dead end. Marissa had turned her phone off. Little did she know, I had her address listed in her contact information, and with today's technology, all I had to do was touch the link, and a map would lead me straight to her.

Well, it would if she lived at Sherry's Bridal Boutique. Next option.

I didn't care if he was pissed at me or if he never wanted to speak to me again—he wasn't about to have a choice. I jabbed my finger into the screen over Foster's name and listened to it ring through the speaker.

Voicemail.

Hell no.

I tried it again. And again. Each time, my call ended with an automated message instructing me to leave my name and number. Fuck that. Fuck all this. I hopped back into the car while the ringing through the stereo continued.

"Oh my God, who died?" At least I could count on Todd to pick up.

"What? No one."

"You never call. In fact, I'm convinced you'd text 9-1-1 if you could."

I rolled my eyes, uninterested in wasting time discussing my disdain for speaking on the phone. "Whatever. I'm driving. Listen…do you happen to have your laptop with you?"

"Oddly enough, I do. Figured it wouldn't hurt to have in case the mood for a saucy video struck."

"Ew." I shook my head, hoping to rid my thoughts of his porn-fest. "Don't ever tell me shit like that again."

"Like you don't give me a detailed rundown of your trysts…"

I didn't have time for this, so I simply cut to the reason for my call. "Anyway, can you look through Marissa's file and see if you can find an address? The one she gave me doesn't exist."

"Then how do you expect me to find it?"

"Gee, I don't know, Todd. You're an investigator… investigate it."

"I'm on a hot date."

As if I cared. "Would you rather take some time to dig this information up for me, or spend a few years behind bars for being implicated in a murder?"

"What? Why would I be…*ohhh*? What happened? I thought everything was copacetic when you refunded her money."

"Long story. Not nearly enough time to tell you now. Just get the address." And with that, I disconnected the call.

Following the directions of Siri, I pulled up in front of Foster's house within ten minutes. His truck was in the driveway, so he had to be home. Granted, this wasn't the day to make assumptions, since the universe was hell-bent on proving them wrong. Yet that didn't stop me from parking along the curb and stomping my way up the front yard, which I had to admit was decorated with stunning landscape work.

After a few hard hits of my fist against the door, it swung open, showcasing a very bitter, very shirtless, *very* sexy man. "What? Don't like it when the tables are turned?"

"Not particularly, but that's not why I'm here."

He leaned against the doorframe with his massive arms crossed over his bare chest. "Then tell me, Poodle. Why are you here?"

"I need Marissa's address." Oddly enough, this was the first time I realized they didn't live together. How I was a private investigator was anyone's guess. But in my defense, having Foster involved in the case muddled my brain somewhat.

"What for? You two having a girls' night? Plan on sitting around in lingerie, drinking and painting each other's nails while talking about me?"

"No. And as much as I'd love to get into all this with you, now's not the time. There's a certain fuckstick in dire need of being broken…by my fist."

Foster held his hands up and pushed off the doorframe with his shoulder. "Damn. What'd she do to get you all riled up? I haven't seen this level of redhead crazy since you found Suzie's underwear in my room."

Now that he mentioned it…that might've been where the originating cause of my aversion to panties had come from. I'd grabbed them off his bedroom floor and almost had them on before realizing they weren't mine.

I shivered and swallowed the bile creeping up my throat. "Well, for starters, she slashed my tires when leaving Starbucks. Once I had that taken care of, I came home, desperate to put an end to my shitty day, only to discover the word 'whore-hole' and many others spray-painted on the front of my *house*."

"Oh, shit," he whispered. "Listen, I'm sorry, Kamryn. I truly am. But I can't help you. How'd she even know where you live? Do you give out your address to anyone who hires you? That's probably not wise."

"I know, which is why I have a PO box. I have no idea how—" The lightbulb over my head flashed brightly. "I gave her a check today. My address is at the top."

"And you're sure it's her?"

"Who else would it be? Who else would've slashed my tires after seeing us together? Was it you?"

"Me? Hell no."

"Okay, then. Marissa's the only one left."

A cocky smirk tugged one corner of his lips. "You sure you haven't pissed anyone else off? Maybe fucked with someone else by sleeping with him only to laugh in his face when it was over?"

His words were like daggers shot clear through my entire chest, with an added punch in the gut for good measure. They caused me physical pain while leaving me speechless.

Before I could say anything, defend myself in some way, my phone vibrated in my hand. And as much as I wanted to ignore the call, use the device as a weapon against Foster and his hateful words, it was Todd. I couldn't send him to voicemail.

"Hey. Did you find it?" I asked, although I got no response. "Hello? Todd?"

"Service is spotty here for some reason." Foster pointed to my cell.

Pulling it away from my ear, I noticed the tiny signal bar at the top, right before "call failed" flashed across the screen. I groaned in frustration, desperate to end this nightmare of a day.

He held the door open wider and stepped aside. "Come in. You can use my landline."

I wanted to make a comment about the nineties calling, asking for their house phone back, but I thought that might come across as ungrateful, and I couldn't risk him kicking me out before I got the information I needed.

There was a chance Todd wouldn't answer without recognizing the number. But to my surprise, it rang twice before his voice flooded the line. "Where the hell are you calling me from?"

"It doesn't matter. Were you able to get the address or not?"

"No. But I got you something better."

I sat in the recliner in Foster's living room, making sure I didn't leave him with an option to get too close. Not while I still felt the effects of his tongue-lashing. "What could possibly be better than what I'd asked for, Todd?"

"First of all, watch the attitude, will ya? Second of all, why didn't you tell me she vandalized your house?"

"It wasn't important at the time."

"Not important? Girl, you have the words, 'Kam's had more wieners than Nathan's hot dogs,' written on your garage door. By the way...she spelled wieners wrong. But we can deal with that later. It should be an easy fix."

"Todd!" I shouted into the receiver, hoping he'd shut up long enough to listen to me. "I'm not keeping it there. Clearly. But after spending all day dealing with the tires she slashed, I decided to hunt the bitch down instead of spending more time dealing with the giant pink penis on my front door."

"Hold up. She slashed your tires, too? What is she...a beast? That's not an easy thing to do." The asshole sounded impressed.

"Get on with it, Todd. You said you got me something better than her address."

"I stopped by your house to get her paper file because that's where I put the photocopy of her driver's license, which is also how I saw the artwork. A little heads-up would've been handy."

"So, you're calling to tell me the address on her license?"

"No. I haven't gotten it yet."

"Then why the hell are you calling me?" My patience had long since vanished by this point. I chanced a glance at Foster, who sat on the couch opposite me with a stoic, emotionless expression on his face. "You said you have something…what is it?"

"Oh, Mrs. Jones across the street came home and saw the mess, so she quickly checked the security footage from the front of her house. She came out when I pulled up and told me she caught it all on camera. The cops were already called and are on their way."

I sighed, my shoulders rolling forward as the first sign of something good came about. "Thank you. I'll be there soon to deal with it. I need to get it cleaned up before Charlie comes home."

"I'm already on it, boss. It's a good thing you called while I was with Jeff. He's a painter, and when he saw the damage, he called his guys out. They'll obviously wait until the cops finish their thing, but it should be all gone before you go to sleep tonight."

"Thanks, Todd. I owe you one. And tell man bun thanks for me, too."

"Will do. See you soon."

I hung up and set the phone on the armrest; then, I dropped my head into my hands to collect myself.

For such a large man, Foster certainly knew how to keep quiet while moving around a room. He was on the sofa one second and perched on the edge of the table in front of me the next. His warm palms on my thighs erased every ounce of anguish over the events of the day, while simultaneously filling me with unanswerable questions.

When I lifted my head and found the agony in his eyes, I nearly lost it. But not as much as when he took my face in his hands and brought his mouth closer to mine. At the last second, I turned away, offering him my cheek —which he didn't take. Instead, he hesitated, and with minimal force, he directed me to look at him again with only his thumb beneath my chin. The same thumb he then used to graze my lips.

But that was all he did. Once he finished studying my mouth, he began to pull away. Something in me snapped. I needed him. I wasn't sure what would come of it, or how he'd handle it, but I crushed my lips to his in a bruising kiss. He stilled for a second but quickly took the lead.

The kiss turned frantic, and I realized I needed this man and all he could offer me. I needed to forget everything that had happened today and just get lost in him. And when he gripped my hips firmly, using his hold on me to slide me off the recliner and into his lap, I knew he'd give me everything I wanted—as well as things I wasn't aware I needed.

He stood, taking me with him, my legs wound around his waist. I didn't care where he took me, as long as he did. I was only in the air for a few seconds before we collapsed onto the sofa with me, straddling his thighs. As if someone had started a timer, we began to rip at each other's clothing, ravenously trying to get the other naked. It shouldn't have been easy with the way we were sitting, and maybe it wasn't, but it seemed we'd both tore off our clothes in a matter of seconds.

Foster twisted to the side until he was on his back, and then yanked me up his body, sitting me on his face. I cried out the instant his mouth covered my clit. I was so turned on that I could feel my juices drip down my thighs. He gripped my ass firmly, forcing me to ride his tongue. I'd lost all inhibitions. He was unyielding in his pursuit of my orgasm, and he didn't disappoint. I came in his mouth, screaming his name.

I was spent from that orgasm, but before I had a chance to come down from my high, Foster slid me down his body and impaled me from below. I screamed out from the sudden intrusion, yet he gave me no time to recover. He was relentless, fucking me hard and fast. I finally caught my breath and started working my hips in rhythm with his. He kept me close, not looking at me— this wasn't anything other than pure, carnal fucking.

I pushed against his chest, needing leverage to see his face as he came, but before I could sit up enough, he shoved me to one side, against the back of the couch, while he rolled out from under me in the other direction, all in one swift move. Before I could figure out what he'd done, he had me on all fours, the leather cushion pressed against my cheek, and drove into me from behind. Our left legs were tangled together where he'd made room for his knee, while he steadied himself with his other foot flat on the floor next to the loveseat.

His thrusts were harsh and punishing as if proving something to me—or maybe to him; I wasn't sure. He grabbed my hair and yanked my head back and to the side, gaining access to my neck. He devoured it, biting and sucking hard. He let go and carefully pushed against my shoulder blade, forcing my face into the cushion once more. It was the push and pull I needed, I craved, the kind of euphoria that had the ability to cleanse the ugliness of the day away. I had never been fucked like this—brutal and hot—and I couldn't get enough. I met him thrust for thrust in my quest for another orgasm.

Suddenly, I felt a dribble of wetness hit my asshole, and then the slightest pressure from Foster's finger rubbing circles around the tight ring of muscle. I tensed at first; I hadn't tried that in years, but honestly, I was so turned on he could have shoved his dick in my ass, and I wouldn't have cared.

Before I knew it, he pushed his finger past the

muscle, and it felt amazing—*beyond* amazing. He worked it in rhythm with his cock before inserting another. I felt like such a dirty whore, but I loved every second of it! The intense pleasure I felt from the combination of his fingers and his cock was like nothing I'd ever experienced.

"Foster, I'm going to come." At those words, he slapped my ass three times in quick, harsh blows, and I came harder than ever before. A few more thrusts and Foster fell over the edge, too. He stilled inside me and came with a guttural moan. We stayed like that for a moment before he pulled out of me and left the room. I collapsed on my stomach, desperately trying to catch my breath, not at all caring where he had disappeared to. And less than a minute later, he came back with a damp cloth and cleaned me up.

"I don't know what I was thinking, Kam." Once again, he reminded me of my place in his world with a few simple words. "Please tell me you're on the pill." It took a minute for it to register that we hadn't used protection.

"Yeah, I am." I noticed that Foster was already getting dressed, which officially doused the moment in ice water. I shifted to my side and pushed myself into a seated position to reach my clothes, refusing to look at him…or speak.

"You should probably be at your house when the

cops show up." He tossed me my shirt and then grabbed his off the coffee table.

Still, I didn't respond. I hated myself for allowing this to happen once again. Knowing how he was in the past, and how he'd been toward me all week—hot and cold, needy and then dismissive—I should've known better. Unfortunately, it seemed I would never learn my lesson where Foster Montgomery was concerned.

We both managed to get dressed in silence, the only sound was his car keys as he lifted them off the table near the front door. I wanted to ask where he was going, but I didn't have the right, nor did I care anymore. He'd made his point known. Now I just had to learn how to be strong when it came to him.

I wasn't foolish enough to believe this would be the last time I'd ever see him, so after leaving his house, on the way to my own, I mentally prepared myself for the next time. I recited easy rejections, ones I would be able to recall in my time of need, and gave myself the most pathetic pep talk.

Red and blue lights flashed in front of my house when I pulled up. And on the driveway with two police officers stood Todd and a man with a bun—Jeff, otherwise known as "man bun."

It seemed the officers already had what they needed, so a few minutes after I arrived, once they had my information and statement, they left. That's when Jeff's crew all piled out of two white vans parked along the road and then unloaded professional painting gear from the backs.

Had I not been so focused on what they were doing, I would've noticed Foster standing with Todd, talking in hushed tones while pointing toward the house. The sun had started to fade, leaving a dusky glow in the sky, just enough to see where to paint as long as the job was finished quickly.

"Come on, Poodle. Let's get you inside and calmed down." Foster took my hand and led me to the front door, and I blindly followed. He waited while I unlocked the deadbolt, and then escorted me to the kitchen table.

"Why are you here?" I asked as he filled a cup with water. I didn't want water, but I also wasn't in the mood to make coffee. Dear Lord...you know it's bad when I don't have the energy to get up and make a pot of the good stuff.

"Just because I'm hurt by what you did doesn't mean I won't be there for you when you need me."

He set the glass on the table and took the seat next to me.

"We need to talk, Kamryn. What you did to me with Marissa was..." He shook his head and stared at his folded hands in his lap. "It was wrong. I deserve better than that. But for now, I'll settle for an explanation."

I pulled my feet to the edge of the chair and hugged my knees to my chest. I wasn't sure where to begin, but he was right; this needed to happen. A talk was long overdue. "As cliché as it sounds…it's not what you think. I didn't purposely go after you."

"No? Look me in my eyes and tell me you never meant to hurt me."

I couldn't because it would be a lie. But I met his stare anyway, only instead of repeating his words, I offered the truth. "I did want to hurt you, selfishly. The opportunity arose to get back at you for the way you treated me back in high school, so I took it."

He shook his head and held up one hand to stave me off. "First of all, how did I treat you? Because the way I remembered it, you didn't have a problem with our arrangement back then."

"You used me and then ignored me, over and over again. You would hook up with me and then forget I existed the very next day. Do you know how humiliating that was, to be treated that way by your best friend's brother? Someone I had to see on a regular basis and know the things you did with Suzie when you'd choose her over me?" I was talking a little louder than I intended, but I was so worked up. He had no clue, no fucking clue.

Foster covered my hand with his on top of the table and waited until my eyes found his. "I didn't ignore you because I wanted to—trust me, that was the *last* thing I wanted. I had to force myself to pretend you weren't in the room when all I could think about was your lips or how your skin pebbled when I touched you. I knew what it would do to your friendship with Dana, as well as the things people would say if they knew about us. I'm well aware of how I was back then. Saying I wasn't the most popular guy in school would be an understatement. I was a complete loser—the weird, hairy, redneck kid. What do you think would've happened if I had walked up to you in the hallway and kissed you in front of everyone?"

As much as it pained me to admit it, he did make a valid point. "I honestly never thought of it that way."

"And I never imagined you wanted more."

I decided to continue, feeling more confident about where this was headed. "I hated how you'd be all over me in private and then snub me the second Suzie would snap her fingers. The first night you kissed me, I woke up the next morning excited to see you. But you walked in like you didn't know who I was and then spent the afternoon in front of me with Suzie. Do you have any idea how that made me feel? Honestly, it took me years to get over the damage caused by the way you treated me. I was so self-conscious, always thought there was something wrong with me because I was only good enough for you as long as we were behind closed doors."

"Are you kidding me? All I wanted was to tell everyone that I got to kiss you. That you let me touch you. I wanted the world to know that you were mine— except you weren't. I always thought *you* were the one who was ashamed of *me* and didn't want anyone to find out."

There was no way to know how much of this was the truth and how much was Foster just telling me what he thought I wanted to hear. But it didn't matter anymore, because the damage had been done, and there was no turning back. "I wish I could believe that, but you did it again this time. At the bar, I smiled at you, and then you turned around like I didn't exist. And then the second we were in the hallway near the bathrooms, where no one could see us, you practically attacked my mouth. A girl can only take so much before she starts to wonder what's wrong with her...again."

"Fuck, Kam. No. That's not how it was at all. If you smiled at me, I didn't see it. I noticed you out there dancing with my sister, and the next time I saw you, you were walking by my table, flirting with one of my boys. That's why I kissed you...to remind you of where your head should be. And I had to wait until Dana wasn't up your ass. Otherwise, she would've flipped her shit."

I took a deep breath and blew it out slowly, wondering how different things would've been had we talked about this when it happened versus letting it build and fester into something more. "That's why I avoided you. I couldn't go through that again. I was finally confident in my own skin, only to doubt myself after one night with you. It wasn't worth it, not after I'd come so far."

"All because I turned around when you smiled at me?"

"No. I mean, yes…but not *only* because of that. You left my house Monday night, and then I didn't hear from you again until Wednesday morning."

He dropped his chin to his chest and huffed. "I'd left my phone at home by accident. I stopped by after work, but you weren't here. And when I got back to the house, the internet wasn't working, so my texts wouldn't go through."

"And there was no other way to get ahold of me? You have a landline."

"Which is all powered by the same company as my internet provider. Which means I had no house phone, no Wi-Fi, and shitty service on my cell. You made it clear you didn't want me around your daughter, so I respected that and stayed away, knowing that if you were home, she would be, too."

His plausible excuses were really starting to grate on my last nerve.

"Anyway, that's why I decided to take the case. Why I tried to get back at you—for all that. When I opened Marissa's email and recognized your picture, I thought it would be easy. I figured it'd give me the chance to make you feel a fraction of the pain you'd caused me."

"I guess I'm just confused as to how Marissa fits into this. How did she find you, and what would she have hired you to do? I doubt she paid you to sleep with me, so what exactly did you think you'd be able to do to get revenge?"

I waited a moment, unsure where the misunderstanding was, but no doubt there was one. "Uh, catch you cheating?" It seemed obvious to me. "That's what she hired me to do. Although you're right, she didn't hire me to spread my legs in order to catch you."

"*Cheating*?" He almost choked on the word. "On who? *Her*?"

"Yeah. Now I'm the one who's confused. Why would you be cheating on someone else?"

"Hell if I know. I'm still not sure how I could've possibly been cheating on her."

"Well, typically…if you are engaged to one woman, and then fuck another woman, that constitutes cheat."

"*Engaged*? Who? Me and Marissa? Is that what she told you?" His shock morphed into amusement. "For real? How much did she pay you?"

"Never mind that. Go back to the engaged part. You sounded a little surprised by that fact."

"Well, yeah. Because I'm not, nor have I ever been, engaged to her. Or to anyone for that matter. I went on one date with that chick. She used to live in the apartment above my buddy. We fooled around at one of his parties, and like a week later, I took her out to dinner. She's bat-shit crazy, so I didn't take her out again. Apparently, she never got the hint. I'm assuming she hired you when she moved out of the complex, no longer able to run into me."

"So, you're telling me she made the whole thing up?"

"Yeah, that's exactly what I'm telling you. I swear, Kam…I've spent the past six months avoiding her like the plague. She texts and calls me all the fucking time. I've even contemplated changing my number. But to hire an investigator…? That's beyond messed up."

I covered my face with my hands and mumbled, "This day just keeps getting better and better."

"Then maybe it's about time to put an end to it." He slid off the chair and walked away.

My initial reaction was anger, thinking he'd left. But then I replayed our entire conversation in my head and realized assumptions and reactions had caused all this. So rather than expect the worst, I patiently waited for the truth to reveal itself, which happened a few minutes later, when Foster strolled back into the room and helped me out of my seat.

"Todd's friends are almost done. He said he'd handle the rest so you can get to bed." Linking our fingers together, he led me away from the table and toward the staircase. Of course, I followed him without question.

He took me to my bedroom and then proceeded to my dresser to pull out a nightshirt. And with his back to me, he allowed me to change clothes. Without a word, he helped me to bed, adjusted the blankets, and then leaned over with his hands pressed into the mattress for support. "You should rest. You've had a long day."

When he tried to pull away, I gripped him harder. "Stay, Foster. Please, don't leave me." I didn't care that I was begging or what he'd think of me.

He was torn; I could see it in his eyes. I was losing him, and I couldn't let that happen tonight—not after all that had come out today. Finally, he exhaled deeply and gave in. In a quick move, he tugged his shirt over his head and stepped out of his shoes but kept on his jeans. Once he had the light out, he slipped into bed, settling in next to me on his back.

I took a chance and curled into his side with my head on his shoulder and arm over his waist. His body went rigid at first, but thankfully he didn't push me away. Instead, he sighed and welcomed me by curling his arm around my shoulder, holding me to him.

"There is absolutely nothing wrong with you, Kamryn. Nothing. You are stunning, both inside and out. Got it?" He paused for a moment, and when I didn't say anything in return, he tightened his hold on me and kissed the top of my head. "I'm not saying that to make you feel better. It's the truth. It's how I've always felt."

I craned my head back to see his face and then kissed him softly. There really wasn't any other way to respond. I had strong feelings for Foster, but I wasn't quite sure I would've called it love. I hadn't ever allowed myself to contemplate that idea because all my time with him had been smothered in a cloud of hurt and made-up betrayal.

He slipped his fingers into my hair and deepened the kiss. I couldn't take it anymore and pulled myself on top of him, straddling his waist. With nothing more than the late evening sky offering little light to my room, I slipped my hands down his chest and unbuckled his belt. He did nothing to stop me; instead, he remained motionless, watching me as if he were trying to memorize this moment. He lifted his hips so I could pull down his jeans, and then he kicked them the rest of the way off.

While he rid me of my shirt, I rubbed my wet pussy up against his length. I didn't need time to prepare for him, as if I'd always been ready for Foster, so I positioned his shaft right where I wanted him and sank down.

We watched each other while we cherished our last moment of togetherness. I wouldn't have called it making love, but honestly, that's how it felt. It was sensual and slow. We took our time, touching and feeling and just being with each other. We climaxed together and stayed in each other's arms for what seemed like an eternity.

I lay there after my body had come down from my orgasm, mindlessly tracing invisible circles on his shoulder with my fingertip, I said, "I don't want to fall asleep. Because I know once I do, this will all end. It'll all be over, won't it?" I whispered with my face nearly buried into the crook of his neck while I held onto him like he were my last breath.

He shifted to his side so that we were facing each other, and without releasing me, he pressed a kiss to my temple.

"We have unmistakably done the worst job of communicating our feelings from the beginning. There's no question about that. I've had strong feelings for you since I first met you. You were always there, and I think I took advantage of the fact that you would be since you were Dana's best friend. Having you back in my life has been amazing. You're fun to be with, and the sex is off the charts, but honestly, I feel like you aren't ready for a serious relationship. The current situation aside, you haven't been single long, and you were with your ex for a really long time, so I think you need some time to explore yourself before you find someone to settle down with again—whether it be with me or someone else. I just want you to be happy." His voice was soft and full of sadness.

I winced at his words, and a tear slipped free because I knew he was absolutely right—I was only just starting to find myself. I wanted to yell at him and tell him he didn't know what I needed or wanted, but I truly wasn't ready to be in a relationship just yet. Maybe that was why I'd found Foster so appealing. Deep down, I knew he wouldn't get attached because he already was. Regardless, none of that made the ache in my chest any better. "I really fucked things up, didn't I?"

He kissed my forehead and pulled me impossibly close. "I think we both did. Right now is not the greatest time to tell you, so I'll hold back, but I need you to know that my feelings for you are strong. I never wanted to come between you and Dana, so I always kept my emotions hidden. But with you, it was always more than something physical. And when the day comes that you're ready for more, I won't make that same mistake again. Okay? I'll be all in, but I can't do that until you're all in, too."

He kissed my forehead.

"I'm sorry, Kam, but I need all of you. I deserve that much. And until you're ready, we'll just have to be friends. I'm okay with that, as long as you are. Now that I've truly had you, I can't imagine my life without you in it."

"You think we can just be friends?" I pulled my head back and stared into his eyes. "Do you think we can be around each other without winding up naked?" It was a serious question because so far, we hadn't been able to do so.

"Of course. I didn't say it'd be easy or even fun at times, but I don't want to lose you. I'll take you however I can get you." He ran his thumb over my cheekbone, never taking his eyes off mine. "But if that's not what you want, then—"

"No, Foster. It is. I mean…it's not, but I think you're right, it's all I can do right now." That was as much as I could say until I had a chance to discover what this was that I felt for him. I was too old, had been through too much, to call it love blindly. For all I knew, it was the after-effects of decades of resentment finally being resolved. But I would figure it out. No matter how long it took me, I would look deep into my soul and discover what these feelings truly meant.

"I've missed you, Poodle," he whispered.

I giggled, finally feeling some lightness take over. "I hate that nickname."

"I love it." He slipped his hand between our bodies and teased me with his finger. "I felt like the luckiest son of a bitch back then. That bush let me know that no other guy had seen it the way I had. You didn't worry about what it looked like, not taking the time to shave it or anything, because you weren't flashing it all over town like some of the other girls in school. It was all mine. And that nickname reminds me of a time when I could pretend, even for a couple of hours, that you felt for me what I had felt for you."

"Well, hell." I sighed. "How do you do it, Foster? How is it that you can call me Poodle because I had a bushy pussy, and I somehow swoon?"

"Magic, baby." He lifted my leg and curled it over his hip, opening me up to him. He'd already been inside me twice today—in the last couple of hours—though I couldn't deny him round three. I wasn't sure when I'd get the chance to be with him again, and I wasn't about to put an end to it before we had to.

I wasn't sure what time we had finally fallen asleep, but when I awoke to the sun shining through my bedroom window, he was gone. His clothes were no longer scattered on the floor, and his phone and keys were absent from the nightstand. But I didn't get up. Instead, I remained in bed and let my pillow soak up my tears until I had to lock it down.

EPILOGUE

"ARE YOU SERIOUS? MY FUCKING BROTHER?" Dana looked like she might actually throw up. It was incredibly fun to watch. "Kam, that's so disgusting. Like beyond fucking gross. I don't even know what to say right now. Foster is…well…my brother. I know every nasty thing there is to know about him. He used to pick his nose and wipe his boogers all over the furniture. He shit in the bathtub once when we were little."

I couldn't breathe. I was laughing so hard, knee-slapping, belly-aching hysterics. "Dana, come on; he's a grown-ass man. Think about it…if he weren't your brother, you would totally understand. That boy is F-I-N-E *fine*. Like so hot. He fills out a pair of jeans and a Henley like no man, and without them, he's—"

Dana slapped her hand over my mouth, cutting me off with a stern look. "Please, for the love of God, don't finish that sentence. I don't even know how I sat through the whole story—it was like listening to someone being murdered. Fucking horrifying is what it was. That shit's messed up, Kam."

At least she wasn't ripping me a new asshole for keeping this from her.

"Now I understand why you didn't tell me. And to be honest, I really wish you would've kept that shit to yourself. But you still didn't answer anything for me. Like what happened to that Marissa chick?"

I waved her off. Anytime I thought back to that day, I didn't think too much about the havoc that woman had brought on me. Instead, I focused on Foster, and how, without the events of that day, I might've never gotten the answers I needed. "She was arrested, but because the courts were backed up, they ended up offering her community service to get her off the books. A slap on the wrist but still something."

She took a few deep breaths, and then a Cheshire grin graced her beautiful face. "Oh. My. God. I just thought of something. If you married Foster, we could be sisters, like for real. As gross as your story was and how nasty I think he is, *that* would make it all worth it."

Her dramatics had me giggling. "I don't see that happening. He decided that we're going to be *just friends*...at least for now."

"How do you feel about that." Concern marred her features as she leaned toward me.

"I'm not quite sure. I haven't had much time to mull it over." I wasn't completely honest, and seeing as I'd kept so much from her lately, I decided to elaborate. "All right, I lied, it sucks. I don't want just to be friends, but he was right. I'm not quite sure that I'm ready for an actual relationship. So maybe we could give this whole friend thing a go and get to know each other better." I looked down at my coffee and sighed.

"You really like him, don't ya?"

My eyes met hers, and I nodded, the lump in my throat preventing me from speaking. I hadn't realized how much until that moment.

"Well, then you need to figure your shit out girl and get him back so we can be *sisters!*"

I rolled my eyes although I was thinking the very same thing.

THE END

JUST KIDDING...

Give your girl some credit.

You didn't seriously think I'd
leave you hanging like that, did you?

Keep reading…

PART 2

NINE

IT'D BEEN about a week since my confession to Dana; the entire conversation had gone way better than I could've hoped for. She was shocked, but she hadn't flipped the fuck out like I thought she was going to. We'd talked for hours about the past, present, and future —or lack thereof—with Foster.

And as I'd told Dana, Foster and I were still in the friend zone. We'd been texting back and forth, but I haven't seen him in person in almost two weeks, and I had to say I was having a hard time with it. I wanted to see him, but at the same time, I was worried about how things would go once we were in the same room. It was hard enough just texting. I couldn't imagine what it was going to be like being near him and not being able to touch him.

I'd run through different scenarios in my head to figure out where we could go or what we could do as "friends." Every time it led to us sleeping together—well in my mind. I thought it would be a safe bet to do something with Charlie. I wouldn't introduce a guy I was dating to her, but since we were friends, it wouldn't be a problem. Having Charlie there would be a great distraction.

I took the plunge and sent him a text, deciding on a very public place, and he took the bait. I guess we were headed to the zoo this weekend. My stomach was in knots already, my mind racing with what I was going to wear, how things would go. I felt like a teenager, and I needed it to stop immediately.

It's just like hanging out with Todd. I repeated that over and over in my head, hoping I would believe it, except I had never slept with Todd and sure as hell didn't want to. "Ugh!" I groaned as I pulled into the dance studio's parking lot to pick up Charlie.

She looked a little down as she walked out of class. Being in competitive dance meant some days were harder than others, so I tried to brighten her afternoon by telling her about the plans to go to the zoo. She was ecstatic and begged me to allow Tiffany to come with us. Her brown eyes gave me that puppy-dog look, and I couldn't refuse her. Although selfishly, I thought that two bubbly, talkative pre-teens would be even better than one.

Saturday rolled around way faster than I had expected. I was excited to see Foster but also nervous about how things would go. I'd spoken to Charlie about him coming, and she seemed to understand more than I had expected and gave me a *don't bullshit me* look when I said we were just friends. I just rolled my eyes at her and left it at that. I was the mother and didn't need to justify my life choices to her—at least that's what I told myself.

Foster and I had fought over who would drive, and he'd won that battle. I really didn't have a reason to say no, other than I didn't want to be in close quarters with him, which I wasn't about to admit out loud.

The girls were nearly bouncing out of their seats the whole way over, and it didn't stop once we got there; surprisingly, the lot was fairly quiet, and there were only a few people in line. When it was our turn at the ticket counter, Foster handed the lady a few pieces of paper, and she gave us all wristbands with what looked to be dinosaur prints on them.

I lifted my wrist. "What's this for?" I'd never received a wristband at the zoo before.

Foster smiled, looking proud of himself. "They have a dinosaur event going on right now. So, I got the package that will allow us access to it, as well as the monorail, food, and we also get an animal feeding."

Before I could say anything about the fact that he'd paid for us, Charlie piped in.

"Dinosaurs?" She squealed, sounding similar to one of those flying pre-historic birds. The smile on her face made my irritation over the fact that he'd paid melt away. Charlie and her friends had been on a dinosaur kick ever since they started putting out new *Jurassic Park* movies. There was no way for him to know that, but by the way Charlie was looking at him, he'd just became one of her favorite people.

I took a deep breath and swallowed my pride before looking up at him. "Thank you."

He smiled down at me, and I wanted nothing more than to stretch up to kiss him, but I refrained.

Tiffany giggled, and Charlie groaned. "Stop looking at each other like that; it's weird." I turned in time to see Charlie roll her eyes and mutter with a smirk, "Just friends."

Fucking kids and their mouths. I let it go, knowing she had just witnessed the two of us lost in each other for a moment, and it had probably creeped her out.

Being around Foster was going to be harder than I thought, but I pulled up my metaphorical big-girl panties and decided to make the best of this day. Giving myself a little internal pep talk, I told my inner slut to calm down and that I could do this. There was no reason why I couldn't have a platonic relationship with a sexy-as-fuck guy who was amazing in bed. I wanted to slap myself for the thought because, honestly, I was lying to myself.

I shooed the girls. "What are you waiting for? Let's go." The enthusiasm in my voice wavered, but I was sure they didn't notice.

As we entered through the turnstile, Foster rested his hand on the small of my back. He had no idea what that minor touch did to me—or maybe he did. I looked up at him, but his expression was unreadable. Maybe he was just a good friend.

Foster pulled out a map. "Where to first ladies?" He held it out so that the girls could see, and Charlie pointed to the monkeys. He folded the map back up. "Monkeys it is."

I tried to keep my distance without being obvious. I chimed in when the conversation allowed, but seeing as Charlie was with her friend and I was off to the side, it was like we were three separate groups. Foster would come over and say something and I'd take the first opportunity to step out of the space.

By the time lunch rolled around, I was exhausted, and although I was grateful that we had the monorail pass, sitting that close to Foster had me right back to where I had started this morning. The girls sat in the next cart, chatting about everything they'd seen and taking selfies.

Foster nudged my side. "Is everything okay?"

I turned and looked up at him. "Yeah. Why?" I feigned ignorance. I wasn't about to admit how much his presence was affecting me. I agreed to this friendship thing, and I was going to stick with it.

I could see the hurt in his eyes as he said, "I feel like you've been avoiding me all morning."

"I'm sorry." I didn't know what else to say other than those two words.

His brow furrowed. "So, you are dodging me?"

I looked at the animals as we rode by to avoid having to look at him. "No, well, not exactly."

"Hey." His voice was soft as he craned his neck so that I was looking at him. "What's up?"

I decided telling him a little white lie was best for both of us at that moment. "Nothing. I'm just a little tired, and you're aware I'm not an outdoorsy person. I'm sure once I get some food in me, I'll be good to go."

He rested his hand on my thigh. "Okay, let's get you some food."

I wished I could've pulled my leg away like a petulant teenager because the butterflies that took flight with just that small gesture were almost too much to handle.

I could've smacked my daughter when she decided they were too cool to sit with us for lunch, not because I cared but because that left me alone with Foster again. The whole point in going out *with* Charlie was so that I could use her as a buffer. Clearly, using my child wasn't a good idea since she was ditching me at every turn. I glared over at her, although she wasn't paying me any mind. *What a little snot rag* was all I could think.

The conversation was light and easy as things usually were with Foster as long as I kept out of my head. I needed to stop overthinking shit and start acting like I would had I been with Dana or Todd.

Charlie leaned into the aisle and shouted at me,

"You're eating so slow. Let's go, Mom. I want to see some dinosaurs." She was yelling at me from five tables over.

I rolled my eyes. "Don't you love how I only exist when she needs something?"

Foster looked toward Charlie and smiled. "Isn't that her job as a teenager?"

I slapped his shoulder. "Don't side with her, and she's not a teenager…yet."

"Close enough." He shrugged. "We should probably get going. She looks like she's busting at the seams to get moving."

I piled my trash onto the tray, and he went and dumped it into the garbage.

Charlie came up beside me with a mischievous look on her face. "So…"

"So what?" I frowned, unsure of what she was talking about.

She raised her brows suggestively and thumbed over her shoulder. "Foster." She practically sang his name.

"What about him?"

"Mom," she whined, clearly frustrated with me.

"He's pretty good looking. I think you should go for it, Miss James." Tiffany's eyes sparkled with excitement.

I nearly choked on my own spit. Was my daughter trying to set me up? "We're just friends, guys." And then it hit me. "Did you ditch us so that we could be alone?"

"Obvi," they said in unison as they both rolled their eyes.

Were these kids for real? I couldn't help the noise that came from deep within my throat. It was the most unladylike sound I'd ever made. It sounded more like something that would come out of a pig than a human.

"Are you all right?" Foster's concern had me trying to hold in another snort.

"I think she's laughing, but honestly, I can't be sure. She could be having a stroke. You guys get those at your age, right?" Charlie deadpanned; maybe she was serious.

Foster chuckled as he rested his hand on my shoulder. Evidently, he appreciated her humor. I, on the other hand, didn't find her amusing in the slightest. I'd have to have a talk with Charlie when we were alone.

After taking a few deep breaths and glaring at my daughter, I finally looked up at Foster through the tears that had formed from laughing. "I'm fine; thank you. You ready to go?"

He looked down at his watch. "We have a little over an hour to roam around with the dinosaurs before we have our feeding time."

The girls squealed and tugged on me. "Let's go," they said as they tried to pull me out of my seat.

"All right, let's go see some dinosaurs." The false enthusiasm was thick in my tone. I was happy for them, but I was ready to go home.

Foster pulled out his map as we walked, the pre-historic zone was on the other side of the park, but at least it was close to the feeding area. We tried to keep up with the girls as they practically ran, stepping on all the dinosaur prints as they went. I finally gave up and just told them not to get too far ahead.

We flashed our wristbands and entered through gates that led to what felt like we'd just walked into a forest somewhere in the Amazon. There were "beware of dinosaur" signs along the walkway, and you could hear dinosaurs in the distance. The girls clutched each other as they walked and screamed when they heard a roar come from within the bushes to our right. I couldn't see anything, but I had to admit it sounded realistic.

I was looking up at Foster as we were talking when his eyes went wide. I turned around slowly but didn't see anything, then out of nowhere, a Velociraptor—I thought that was what it was called—jumped out of the bushes right in front of me. I screamed and nearly knocked over Foster. He pulled me in by the waist. He almost had me forgetting that we were in the middle of fucking *Jurassic Park* except for a freaking Tyrannosaurus —that one I knew for sure—came running after the other dinosaur right in front of us.

My hands gripped Foster's arm as my heart raced. It wasn't real, but these things looked like genuine pre-historic beings walking around before our eyes.

Charlie ran over to us. "Did you see that, Mom? That was so cool." She was snapping selfies as she spoke.

"Yes, I'm not sure you could miss a twenty-foot-tall dinosaur running." My heart was finally calming, so I reluctantly let go of Foster's arms, and he dropped one of his hands from my waist but kept the other on the small of my back as we walked.

The rest of the excursion through the jungle wasn't as entertaining, I was glad to say. I was a little more prepared when an animal leaped out of nowhere now that I was on high alert, but I still jumped and squealed slightly.

I finally let down my guard once we walked out of the exit gate and into the dinosaur gift shop. Although I said no, Foster bought both the girls some souvenirs, and they both hugged him like he was the best thing since sliced bread.

I didn't want him to think he had to buy them anything. "You didn't have to do that, you know?"

"I know. I wanted to." His eyes flickered down to my lips and back up to meet my gaze.

I knew that look, and it took some real restraint not to reach up and kiss him.

He closed his eyes for a moment before opening them again. "Who's ready to feed some penguins?" And there went the moment, that really wasn't a moment, but I was calling it a moment.

The girls were excited about the feeding, and honestly, so was I. I'd never been that close to a penguin, and they were adorable from a distance, so I couldn't wait.

As we walked toward the exhibit, Charlie turned to

Foster. "So, are you dating my mom?" She stared up at him, waiting for a response as I tried to hold back the burst of laugher that was dying to explode out of me.

Foster looked to me for help, but I was letting him take the lead on this one. I just shrugged and waited to hear what he would say.

"No, we're just friends." The bastard smiled smugly, and my daughter, who literally never left anything alone, didn't push and ran ahead of us. *Ugh.*

He put his arm around me and pulled me in to whisper into my ear, "Should I have told her all the dirty things I've done to you and how I still think about doing them every waking hour?"

I swallowed hard, not able to speak.

"I didn't think so." He kissed my forehead and chuckled.

Charlie yelled for us to hurry up, and I pulled out of Foster's arms. I didn't want her to get the wrong idea. Although we both *thought* about more, we truly were just friends right now.

When we entered the gate, we had to step into a rain suit, boots, and rubber gloves before we entered the exhibit. The zookeeper led the way into the area. Although the rain suit wasn't warm, I was glad for the extra layer since it was quite cold in there. All the penguins were on the other side of their swimming pool, walking around on the rock wall. Everyone in our group started pointing and talking about how cute they were.

Charlie, of course, continued snapping selfies. The zookeeper handed us each a small bucket and explained how the feeding would take place, along with the dos and don'ts.

We were all intently listening when Charlie interrupted her, "We have to hold a fish?"

The horrified look on her face had me in stitches. The zookeeper looked up at me with furrowed brows. I immediately stifled my laughter like a scolded child.

She turned her attention back to my daughter. "Yes, that would be the only way you'll be able to feed the penguins. If you are not comfortable with that, I can have a coworker take you outside." She didn't seem too impressed by the disruption.

Charlie's cheeks pinked as she shook her head without saying another word.

As soon as we took hold of the fish, the penguins started to dive into the water toward us. There were so many, and they came from all directions. It was really cool to watch. I was a little freaked out when one came up and took the fish from me and then one from Foster, but after eating them, he just sat there—wait, did penguins sit? Their ass is so close to the ground, I wasn't sure they did. Do they even have knees? I was going to have a lot of googling to do later.

I reached down and fed him another fish just as the zookeeper came over. She ran her hand down the back of the penguin I was feeding. "This is Chitti. He doesn't usually like anyone. He likes to eat and run."

I puffed out my chest, feeling proud that this little guy seemed to like me.

"You can pet him if he'll let you. No sudden movements and run your hand slowly like this." She ran her hand down him again to demonstrate. I pulled off my glove and reached out. The feel of his feathers nearly had me pulling my hand back. I'd expected him to feel like a bird, but it was slicker than I'd anticipated. That shouldn't have come as a surprise, seeing as it was a penguin and they *swim*. I mentally slapped myself while simultaneously patting myself on the back for not voicing any of my contemplations out loud.

Foster nudged me in the side. "This is pretty cool, huh?"

"It really is." Looking over at Charlie and Tiffany laughing as they interacted with the penguins who'd gathered around them, I couldn't help but smile. "Thank you for this. I had no idea you could even do anything like this."

"Any time. I had a great time with you guys today. I'm glad we could do this." The corners of his eyes crinkled as he gazed down at me.

"Me too."

We all piled into Foster's truck, and my feet sighed in relief. They weren't used to being used for that long of a time period. It had been a long day, and I was sure everyone was exhausted.

Tiffany's phone chimed with an alert. "My mom says she'll pick us up in an hour and take us for dinner if that's okay."

I turned to Charlie. "Us?" This type of stuff irritated me. "Why do you always do this? You need to start asking me in advance instead of springing stuff on me at the last second." I tried not to raise my voice, which was a task in and of itself. I was a yeller, and reigning it in was difficult, to say the least.

"Oh, did I forget to tell you that I was sleeping over?" She stared at me with pleading eyes. "Can I please?"

I huffed out a breath to calm myself and gritted my teeth before speaking. "More like you forgot to *ask* me."

Foster chuckled under his breath. "Hey, Kam, your redhead temper looks like it's about to surface."

I wanted to throat punch him for thinking this was funny.

Charlie giggled and thumbed toward him. "This one's a keeper."

"We're just friends. Jesus. And he'll be lucky if he remains my *friend* because I'm about to slap both of you upside the head." I contemplated telling her no, but then thought about how I just wanted to relax and do nothing, which wasn't fair to her to keep her from having fun. Sighing, I gave in. "I guess you can stay over, but you better get all your homework done while you're there."

The smile that graced her beautiful face was stunning. "I already did it." She really was a good kid.

"Okay, then I guess just have fun."

"Thanks, Mom." She blew me a kiss since she couldn't get out of her belt to give me one. "Love you."

"Love you too."

The girls' giggles and whispers were the only things heard on the ride home, and the moment I unlocked the front door, they raced off to Charlie's room to get ready for their sleepover.

Foster followed me into the kitchen. "Looks like she's going to miss you."

I rolled my eyes. "She's devastated." The refrigerator called my name as my stomach rumbled. The sight of leftover lasagna was like a beacon of light beckoning me. "Do you want anything to eat?" I didn't look back at Foster before starting to make my plate and setting it in the microwave.

"Sure, what you got there?" He leaned over my shoulder, way too close for comfort.

"Lasagna. I'm not cooking, sorry."

He hummed his satisfaction into my ear, and his breath fanned across my cheek. "Lasagna is always better as leftovers anyway."

I quickly turned to face him, not thinking of how

close he was. His nose was a mere inch from mine. I swallowed hard, trying to remember what I was going to say. "Isn't it?"

"Knock, knock."

I jumped at the sound of Jessica's voice as she called out from behind us. I whirled around, and she was standing in the kitchen doorway, eyeing Foster.

I swallowed hard and cleared my throat. "Hey, Jess. Uh. Um. The girls are getting Charlie's stuff together upstairs." I watched her as she seemed to be focused solely on Foster.

She seemed to snap out of her daze and finally looked at me with a huge grin. "Hey, how was the zoo?" Her eyes flicked between Foster and me.

"It was really good. I'm sure they will talk your ear off about it, and with the number of photos they took, it'll feel like you were right there with us."

She rolled her eyes and shook her head. "Oh great, you sure you two don't want them to stay here with you?" She knew exactly what I meant. Our girls could chatter on for hours.

"Hey, don't bring me into this. I'm not staying, so this is between y'all." Foster's deep voice drew our attention to him.

Jessica's brow rose as I'm sure she doubted his statement, but she didn't voice her question. Instead, she just smirked and muttered, "Well, that's a bummer."

"We're ready," Tiffany sing-songed as she ran down the stairs with Charlie in tow. "Can we go now? I'm starving."

The microwave dinged, and I pulled out my hot plate. "We have leftover lasagna if you'd like?"

Tiffany shook her head. "No, thank you, we're going out, right, Mom?"

"That's the plan. You two have a good night. Thanks for bringing her along today." Jessica smiled at me.

"Any time." I gave Charlie a stern look. "You be good and mind your manners." I could tell she was dying to roll her eyes, but she refrained.

"I will. Love you." She came around to hug me and gave Foster one, too, throwing me for a loop. She looked up at him with a huge smile. "Thanks for taking us today. That was the best."

Foster didn't seem thrown at all as he hugged her back. "You're very welcome. I had a lot of fun, too."

Charlie walked off without a second glance, and Tiffany followed behind.

Jessica looked at me with wide eyes. "I'll be texting you later." It sounded like a warning. I guess now I'd be prepared.

"Have fun," I shouted after her.

Foster grabbed his plate and started to get his food ready. "That was weird."

I wasn't sure what to say. "Wasn't it? Charlie's not

really affectionate, so I'm sorry if that made you uncomfortable."

He started the microwave before turning back to me. "I didn't mean Charlie. I was talking about Tiffany's mom. Why would a hug have made me uncomfortable? Should I be?"

I took a bite of my food as I tried to process the conversation and how to continue it. "I guess not. I just assumed that you would be. Most guys would feel awkward is all." I should've known to expect something different from Foster. "Forget I said anything. Jessica isn't usually weird; she's obviously wondering who you are and is going to have mega questions to ask me, I'm sure."

He sat down beside me with his plate. "Why are women so weird? Can't two people of the opposite sex be friends without people assuming we're sleeping together?"

I shrugged. "Maybe because it's not something that happens often. I mean, we *have* slept together more than once." I left out the part about how I'd love to sleep with him again over and over and wouldn't mind taking him upstairs right now.

"True, but not since then we've become strictly platonic friends."

I didn't say anything; instead, I continued eating my dinner in silence. I hated it when he talked about us just being friends. I needed to get my feelings in check because my mind and heart and vagina were all on different pages.

Foster had taken my plate when I was done and tidied up, even though I had insisted I could do it. He came back around the counter and leaned up against it, looming over me where I sat. "Any big plans this week?"

He seemed so at ease like this entire friendship thing wasn't fazing him at all. I, on the other hand, was going insane. I needed him to keep his distance, but I also wanted him close. Ugh, what was wrong with me? *Get a grip.*

Although my libido was going crazy, I took a calming breath and decided to get my shit together. Smiling a fake smile, I responded, "Nothing. What about you?"

"Well..." He turned his body toward me. I held my breath and crossed my legs as his scent was not helping my situation. "I was hoping you'd do me a favor."

Anything for you. It was the first thing to come to mind, but I didn't dare say that out loud. "What's that?"

"I have a charity event that I have to go to for my company. I hate these black-tie events with these stuck-up rich folks, but it's also a great cause as it's for *Big Dog's Haven.* I would love it if you came. We could people watch, which I know you love to do and drink and dance. What do you say?"

Ugh, a night out with Foster in a *suit*? How would I survive that? "Sure, sounds like fun," I lied. It was going to be torture, but I was going to get the best dress ever. "When is it?"

"Next weekend."

"That works since Charlie will be at her dad's house. Text me all the details, so I don't forget." Like I'd forget something like this.

TEN

I'D GONE to every store I could think of this week, and nothing had that wow factor I was searching for. I wanted to look amazing, and nothing worked. I hated shopping for clothes and felt completely defeated, so I called for reinforcements.

Todd walked into my closet. "Okay, I know that you hate this, but tomorrow is a huge deal. This charity event is one of the biggest events of the year. So, I want you to look your best for the cameras. There will be photographers there, of course, so we need something fabulous to pair with the amazing new hair you'll have after your appointment tomorrow." He looked at me with an enormous grin. "And, of course, we want to make that yummy man of yours squirm."

I sat down on the bed with a dramatic sigh. "He's not my man. We're just friends."

Todd looked back at me over his shoulder with a look of distaste. "Girl...I've been in the same room with you two. You could cut the sexual tension with a knife. You guys are both delusional if you think you're ever going to be *just friends*."

Todd actually started throwing my clothes out of the closet and onto my bed. It was like that scene from *Clueless* when Cher was trying to find an outfit for her date minus the computer program and scrolling closet.

Dana walked in, right amidst the chaos. "Who has sexual tension? What did I miss?"

"Red here and your brother."

I tensed, wondering how she'd react, but surprisingly she just laughed. Todd had that effect on people.

She leaned over and hugged me and then sat down beside me. "Hey girl, I see he's working his magic on you already?"

"He better pull a Mr. Clean afterward because I'm not picking all this shit up."

He shouted out from the closet, "Todd doesn't clean, sorry. I'm not charging for my services; the least you could do is pick up after me."

My text alert sounded.

Foster: Are we still on for tomorrow?

My face felt like it was on fire I was smiling so big

Me: Of course

"What's got you all smiles?" Dana asked as she leaned over my shoulder.

I turned my phone slightly away from her. "Does no one understand personal space anymore?"

Todd poked his head out of the closet. "What are you two going on about?"

Dana thumbed toward me. "Kam's Cheshire grin over her texts."

I still wasn't used to being open with Dana about Foster. I wasn't going to keep things from her anymore, but I didn't want to rub it in her face.

Todd smacked his lips. "Oh, that's an easy one. It's got to be Foster. Dana, have you not been in the room with those two together?"

Dana had been in the room with us *many* times, but anyone would've thought we wanted to gouge each other's eyes out, not jump each other's bones.

"Yes, I have, and for as far back as I can remember, I thought they wanted to kill each other, not—" she pretended to gag—"fuck each other." She covered her mouth. "I can't believe I just said that about my brother and my best friend."

"I'm sorry. I bet this is super weird for you. At least now, we're just friends, so you don't have to worry about us *doing* anything like that again."

This time I got *the look* from both of them. I leaned back, feeling judged all of a sudden. "What?"

"*Friends?* What happened to sisters? I'm counting on you, Kam. You're my only hope."

I flopped back onto the bed, snorting with amusement. "You two are ridiculous."

Todd rolled his eyes. "Yeah. We're the ones who are ridiculous. Keep telling yourself that." He went back to my closet, talking shit about my clothes under his breath.

After an agonizing hour of trying on clothes, I was completely drained, but Todd wasn't going to let it end there.

Nope, that wasn't how Todd worked. He sat on his haunches and slapped his thighs on a sigh. "I've exhausted all my options here. I'm afraid you'll just have to go shopping."

I groaned—he knew how much I hated clothes shopping. "I've already been. There's nothing out there." I picked up my phone. "I should just cancel."

"I know, but I'm sending you to my stylist. She'll hook you up. My treat." He looked so proud of himself as he sat up tall.

I wasn't going to argue if Todd was willing to pay. Maybe his fancy stylist could work her magic.

"Whatever, wouldn't want to embarrass my Toddey Woddey, even though you won't even be there." I pinched his cheek and then smacked it playfully.

"Aw, thanks, Kami Wammy, your closet is a disgrace, by the way." He looked around and scrunched up nose as if smelling something foul. "You should probably clean this mess up as well." He was un-fucking-believable.

"You've got to be shitting me."

Todd waved his phone in the air. "All set with Jasmin tomorrow at two, so you'll have to hurry after your hair appointment." He clapped his hands excitedly and jumped up. "I can't wait to see what she picks for you."

"I can," I said under my breath with an eye roll. I was so not looking forward to this.

WE'D SPENT Saturday afternoon at someplace I'd never heard of called *Classy yet Sassy*. To me, the name didn't say high-end charity events, but Todd knew what he was talking about because they had a little of everything. Jasmin picked out a ton of dresses, and they all fit me like a glove. It was so hard to choose.

We'd agreed on a strapless midnight-blue full-length with lace sides for a little sexiness and an open crisscross back for even more. Todd nearly screeched through the phone when I FaceTimed to show him. He made me send Foster a text letting him know I was wearing blue. He sent a text back immediately, asking for a photo that I refused, so he settled for a close up of the fabric, so he knew what color. I didn't think he'd care, but I guess I was wrong once again.

I felt really good about my choice and thought I had a

killer dress. And my hair looked amazing. I loved my new cut—highlights with beach waves—I felt ten years younger.

Todd finished up his appointment with a client just in time to beat me home. The moment I stepped up to the porch, he nearly ripped the door off its hinges to get to me.

"Fabulous." Todd yelped as he opened the door, seeing my hair for the first time. He ran his fingers through it, admiring it from all angles.

I smacked at his hand and ducked away. "Enough, you're giving me a complex."

"But it looks amazing. I can't get over it."

"Wait until you see the dress in person, I had to reign that girl in a bit, but I came out with a killer ensemble for tonight." I was actually looking forward to an evening out.

Todd rubbed his hands together excitedly; he lived for this shit. I made him wait for me to do my makeup and get dressed. He was knocking on the door just as I was zipping up my dress.

"Holy Hannah, you look fabulous." His hand was over his mouth, and I swore I saw a tear in his eye—so overly dramatic.

Todd rarely saw me in make-up since I wore it only for occasions. I'd touched up my already amazing hair. I had to admit that I looked pretty good if I did say so myself.

"Thanks, although I hate to admit it, your store was awesome even though some of it looked like something a hooker would wear."

He laughed because he knew it was true. He held me at arm's length, admiring me. "I just can't get over it." He kissed my cheek. "I better get going before your man gets here."

I smacked him on the side of the head. "Just friends."

He fixed his hair that was still perfect and gave me a look. "Keep telling yourself that, girly. Maybe you'll start to believe it." He blew me a kiss as he walked out the door, shouting behind him, "Have a good time with your *friend*."

I closed the door behind him and paced the room. I hadn't been nervous, but the moment Todd left, I started to panic. Maybe this wasn't such a good idea after all. I started to doubt my dress and my hair.

"Fuck!" I nearly shouted as I jogged toward the bathroom to take a look at what I was working with, but just as I started up the stairs, the doorbell rang. I debated on ignoring it.

Then he knocked.

"Ugh!" I groaned and headed for the foyer. With my hand gripping the knob, I took a deep breath and opened the door.

There Foster stood in his tuxedo looking like he'd walked off a runway. "Holy shit." My voice was merely a whisper.

He closed his mouth as a smile spread across his face. "Holy shit works for me. You look...perfect." Moving forward, he rested his hand on my hip as he leaned in to kiss my cheek before stepping inside. "I hate being the first to these types of things. We could kill some time. Do you want to—"

I stopped him mid-sentence. "Nope, we need to leave now." No way in hell was I going to be able to stand being in this house alone with him dressed like *that*.

His smirk had that damn dimple on full display. "Okay...I was just going to suggest having a beer or something."

Foster had no idea what he was doing to me. I was already squeezing my legs together, and he'd just walked in the door. How was I going to dance with him? I should've taken care of myself before he came over. *Dammit.* "Listen, this whole friend thing might be easy for you, but all I want to do is rip your clothes off right now. And correct me if I'm wrong, but that's *not* what friends do. So I couldn't give a shit if we're early as fuck." I'd decided just to lay it all out and be honest.

Foster was trying not to laugh, but he was failing miserably.

I picked up my clutch off the console table and smacked him with it. "Don't laugh at me."

The dick stepped closer, his cologne invading all my senses. Taking a deep breath to calm myself was a bad idea; it only heightened the effect he was having on me.

Why did he affect me like this? I looked down to avoid eye contact and jumping him.

"We knew this friendship thing wouldn't be easy, Kam, but we both agreed it was for the best and that the ball was in your court." He lifted my chin, so I met his stare. "I am having the same thoughts you are." He raked his gaze down my body. "And then some. I may seem cool and calm on the outside, but don't for one second think that my feelings have changed."

The pull to lean in and kiss him was strong. I wasn't sure how to do this. I wasn't sure if he helped or made things worse, knowing that he still had feelings for me. Either way, it didn't change the fact that my libido was on fire. I blew out a breath. "Beer?"

He smiled and nodded. "Sure." He knew I needed a pass, and I was grateful he was willing to give me one.

The beer helped a little to calm my nerves, allowing me to relax and enjoy his company. Being with Foster was easy when I got out of my head. I just hoped I could stay out of it for the rest of the night.

When we finally walked out the door, I was surprised to find a limousine waiting for us. I cocked a brow at Foster.

He bent over and gestured toward the car. "Your chariot awaits, madam."

"Thank you, kind sir." I giggled and headed toward the open door.

We pulled up to the valet, and I couldn't believe the

opulence around us. I was entirely out of my element with these people, but at least I knew I *looked* the part. Foster came out of my side of the car and linked arms with me. "You ready?"

Looking into his eyes, I realized how much I wasn't. "Not really, but let's do this."

"I promise the people watching will be *more* than worth it."

"A man after my own heart."

The ballroom was a little over the top for my taste— too much detail, and gold was *not* my thing but to each their own. There were a lot of rich people who liked extravagance.

We were shown to our table where we checked out the place cards of the others we'd be seated with. Of course, I knew none of them. Luckily, Foster had sat with a few of them the year before, so he assured me they weren't the stuck-up folks who you could see herding toward each other around the room.

The bar was our first stop to give me some liquid courage to deal with these rich folks tonight. I wasn't sure how much alcohol I needed to deal with people of this caliber, but it was going to be more than I'd usually consume.

Foster leaned toward me, placing his hand at the small of my back. "You know one year they did a bachelor auction, and I stupidly agreed to participate."

"Oh yeah? How was the date?" I didn't really want to know, but I wasn't about to admit that.

He paused for a minute and then chuckled. "I'm not even sure you'd believe me if I told you. She was honestly a complete psychopath, but I have to put up with her. She's big money and has hooked me up with a lot of wealthy clients over the last couple of years. Luckily, I only see her at this event, but trust me, it's more than I wish to handle."

I scanned the room as if I could tell which one it was. "Come on; she can't be that bad."

"Oh, but she is. You'll see I'm sure she won't be deterred just because I have a beautiful woman on my arm." He pulled me in close. "You promise not to leave my side?"

My mouth hung open in mock horror. "I see how it is. You're just using me as a shield tonight. Well, sir, I will have you know that I will not be mistreated like that. I deserve better." I went to pull away, but he tightened his grip and pulled me back in.

"I know we're just friends," his breath against my ear caused a trail of goose bumps to form, "but if we weren't, I'd be bending you over in the coat closet and spanking your ass for that smartass tongue of yours."

A gasp escaped my mouth before I could stop it. I tried to play it cool, although I was feeling anything but. "Is that so?" I swallowed hard and tried to calm my racing heart and heaving chest.

"It is." He pulled back and looked down at me, his eyes blazing with heat.

I was sure I was bright red from the thoughts running through my mind. I cleared my throat and squared my shoulders. "Well, too bad, we are just friends, so there won't be any of that." I tried to sound sure of myself, although I was anything but.

Foster had my mind racing with the possibilities of what he could do to me. I was also grateful I had no clue where the coat closet was because I would most likely be halfway there already.

His body shook with his silent laughter, but I ignored it and took the drink the server offered. He had undoubtedly overheard every word, and like any good bartender, he knew I needed more liquor and kept his mouth shut. He and I were going to become close pals tonight. I thought I would need the alcohol for the snotty rich people, but now I thought Foster might be the main source for my inebriation tonight.

A partition on the other side of the room opened up. "What's that?"

Foster looked up to see what I was talking about. "They have merchants in there who donate a percentage of their sales tonight to *Big Dog's Haven*."

"No, shit? Shopping is my jam." I started toward the vendors like I was being summoned. "Let's go," I called over my shoulder, not waiting for Foster.

"Yes, ma'am." He caught up quickly and placed his

hand on my lower back. With the low-cut design, he got nothing but skin, and it made me want to squirm away to avoid the feelings Foster's touch invoked.

The "shops" were fabulous. Not only did I find some great items, but I couldn't wait to check out their stores. I dropped a few hundred dollars as I continued to justify it to myself by chanting it was for charity over and over in my head.

By the time we got to the silent auction, I was feeling a great buzz from the mimosas they were handing out like water—speaking of water, I needed some.

Between Foster and me, we'd bid on half a dozen items, and if we won them all, we'd be dropping a lot of dough. I secretly hoped that my bids were just helping to drive up the price for a good cause.

Foster grabbed my bags from me and took my hand. "We should take a seat. Dinner will be served soon, and you don't want to miss it. The food is amazing."

"It should be for five hundred bucks a plate." A woman's voice came from behind us.

I nearly spat my drink out at the price of the plate, but when I turned to see a gorgeous redhead who screamed money, I held it in. Foster froze beside me but hadn't turned around yet.

"Foster, darling, how are you?" her sweet voice rang.

His hand gripped mine as he slowly turned around. The smile on his face was fake as he gritted his teeth.

"Salma, how are you?" He pulled me in close and wrapped his arm around my waist protectively.

Just then, it clicked, and I realized this was the psychopath who'd bought Foster in the auction. Reaching out my hand for her to shake, I put on the biggest smile I could muster. "Hi, Salma, I'm Kamryn. Nice to meet you."

She sneered at my hand but took it with the daintiest of shakes. "Charmed, I'm sure."

Did she really just say that? Barely holding in a snort, I looked up at Foster, who I could tell was biting his cheek, trying not to burst out laughing.

The bitch reached her claw up and ran her red-tipped finger down his chest. "Foster," she whined his name. "You better save me a dance."

I tensed, thinking about his hands on her.

He looked down at me with affection. "If Kamryn here ever gives me a rest. She loves to dance this one."

Was he seriously putting this on me? *Fucker.* "We will have to see how much energy I have tonight." I winked and smiled sweetly at her while thinking I'd like to throat punch her.

"I'll see you"—Selma jabbed at Foster's chest with her talon—"later tonight." She then blew him a kiss and turned on her heel.

"Well, that was…thought-provoking." I was going to keep most of my opinions to myself. I knew that she had a big influence on this community and that Foster counted on business from these people. I didn't want to screw that up for him.

Foster pulled me along. "She's something, isn't she?"

Although I wanted to ask if he'd slept with her, I held my tongue. It really wasn't my place. She was a very attractive woman, but even after a moment's interaction with her, anyone could tell she wasn't the type of person you would want to truly associate with—well, at least not in my not-so-rich world.

"Thanks for throwing me under the bus, by the way."

His dimple was on full display as he smirked and pulled out my chair for me. "I've seen you dance around your kitchen like a wild woman, so I'm hoping that you'll stay in my arms all night long."

I wanted the same thing, but my idea of in his arms had a more horizontal meaning than his. "Doubtful. At least she's not haggard. It won't be too bad to dance with her."

Before he could say anything, the other seats at our table started to fill up, and introductions began. Foster was right about these people. They were down to earth and normal. Although they all cleaned up nicely, something that said they weren't stuck-up, rich assholes.

The conversation was engaging, but my eyes couldn't stop wandering to the other redhead in the room. Yet she hadn't noticed the daggers I was throwing her way as her eyes hadn't left Foster.

He leaned in and whispered, "I didn't sleep with her."

"I didn't ask." *Although I wanted to.*

"I know, but by the way you've done nothing but glare at her, I wanted you to know that. Not that she didn't try, and although she may be physically attractive, there's absolutely nothing worthy on the inside—that makes her ugly all-around in my book."

I looked up at him with wide eyes. I wasn't sure why that surprised me since Foster wasn't superficial in any way, but his words caught me off-guard. I guess he'd seen me staring. I couldn't help it. It was killing me that she acted like she owned him. Salma had no idea what our relationship dynamic was, yet she *touched him* like he wasn't standing there with another woman. Something about that grated on my nerves like nothing before.

"She's literally just stared at you throughout dinner and speeches."

He shrugged. "I hadn't noticed."

I turned to him in disbelief. "You really aren't aware of her piercing gaze right now?"

"Nope. I'm too busy watching you." He lifted his glass to his lips and took a sip without looking away from me.

Everyone clapped, and we followed suit, even though I had no idea what we were clapping for.

The master of ceremonies told everyone to enjoy their

night and announced that the available dogs would be joining us on the dance floor shortly.

I backhanded Foster in the stomach. "Shut up! They are going to have dogs up for adoption walking around?" I was beyond excited.

"Yes, I always want to take all of them home. I've always wanted to move to the country and have a big property and just rescue a bunch of animals."

"No way! That would be awesome. I'd love to move to the country, too, but not too far; I still need to be able to shop. But that sounds like a dream." I gripped his forearm. "You should do it. Wouldn't that be good for business too? I'm sure you have some crazy machines for work."

"I do. Right now, I rent a yard, so it would save me money to do it as well. Maybe I'll find the right woman who wants to settle down on a farm full of animals." His shrug said it was no big deal, but the grin that adorned his face told me that he was looking for a reaction from me.

I wasn't about to give him the satisfaction, so I took a sip of my wine and responded as cool as possible. "I'm sure she's out there somewhere. Shit, maybe even in this very room."

He looked down at me with a raised brow, and I nodded in Salma's direction. "Wow!" was all he said as he shook his head.

Visions of a life with Foster became more and more

clear the more I got to know him as a friend. I knew him intimately, and I knew the old Foster, but the grown-up version of him was something I was enjoying discovering. I was also quickly realizing that he was textbook life partner material in more ways than I knew, and if I didn't get my shit together, someone who matched his perfection would most certainly come along and snatch him up.

"Dance with me?" Foster stood beside me with his hand outstretched.

I hadn't noticed him get up while I was fantasizing about him in ways that I hadn't even realized I wanted. When Landon and I had divorced, I didn't think I'd ever want to get married again, but since Foster had come back into my life, my ideal life seemed to have shifted.

I took his hand and followed him onto the dance floor. *If You Leave Me Now* by Chicago came on as he pulled me in close was. Their sound had always been one I had loved growing up. My mother had played the hell out of their albums, and when she didn't have them playing, the radio did.

I hummed the tune as I rested my head on Foster's shoulder. His hand sat on my bare lower back as we swayed to the beat and the whole world melted around us. Being in Foster's arms was one of the best feelings— safe and protected was something I had never felt with Landon. It was more like an arrangement with him.

I lost track of how many songs we'd danced to when

we took a break. Foster grabbed us drinks while I went to the washroom. I couldn't believe I still looked like I did when I left the house. Other than a little lip touchup, I was good to go.

The moment I walked out of the bathroom, I was distracted by the cutest blue-nose pit bull puppy. He was adorable. I wanted nothing more than to take him home, but when I asked, they informed me that he was already adopted. I looked up to find Foster watching me. My smile fell when I saw Salma approach him and rest her hand on his forearm.

Reluctantly I said goodbye to the adorable puppy. "Paws off my man, bitch," I muttered through gritted teeth. I knew It was ridiculous, and I had no real claim over him, but tonight he was with me. So that was enough in my books to get her to back the fuck off.

Foster's eyes were begging me to rescue him. I debated on whether I should let him squirm.

Clearing my throat as I approached, I immediately linked arms with Foster, and he handed me a glass. "Thank you, baby." I took a big gulp of my drink. "All that dancing has me parched."

Foster kissed my forehead. "Me too. Are you ready to get back out there?"

I looked up at him and thought about saying no.

"I think I've been plenty patient. It's my turn." Salma held her drink out. "Hold this for me, would you?"

I wanted to smack it out of her hand, but instead, I

took Foster's glass from him. "I'm sure the bartender will hold yours for you; my hands are full."

Foster pleaded without words, but I wasn't sure what he wanted from me. He couldn't afford for me to be my usual bitchy self since it would most definitely ruin things for him financially, so I just mouthed *I'm sorry*.

I was glad to have a seat that faced away from the dance floor. I wasn't up for watching another woman groping and grinding on Foster.

I'd had two drinks by the time I felt a tap on my shoulder. I looked up to find a handsome older man smiling down at me. "May I have this dance?"

I was reaching out to accept when Foster grabbed my hand and pulled me up and into his side. "Nice try, Lucas, not happening, old man." Foster started to pull me toward the dance floor.

"That was rude." I turned back to apologize, but Lucas had already walked off.

Foster pulled me into him as we stepped onto the dance floor. "You may be okay with me dancing with another woman, but I am *not* okay with you dancing with another man."

I pulled back to look up at him. "Why? We're just friends."

He didn't seem to like that. His brow furrowed. "I know, but..." Letting out a breath, he dropped his forehead to mine. "You know it's not that simple, Kam."

"I'm just fucking with you, and for the record, I

didn't *want* you dancing with her. I wanted nothing more than to tell her to go fuck herself, but I know you have a lot to lose if she were to get pissed off, so I bit my tongue."

His eyes flicked down to my lips and then back up before he leaned in and kissed me on the cheek. "Thank you."

I smiled at him, although I was screaming inside. "Don't expect it to happen often; being a redhead means I can only take so much."

"I'm well aware. Remember, I grew up with two crazy gingers."

The rest of the night went by way too fast; I didn't want it to end. The limo pulled up to the curb, and we climbed in.

Foster rested his hand on my thigh. "Thanks for coming with me tonight."

The heat of his palm distracted me for a moment, but I was able to form the words to respond. "Thanks for inviting me. I had a great time."

"Me too."

I rested my head on his shoulder as we rode through the city. "I guess this friendship thing isn't so bad. I still think friends with benefits would be a lot more fun."

He groaned. "You're killing me; you know that, right?"

I rolled my eyes, knowing he couldn't see me. He was

killing me, but I knew why he was doing this. "Yeah, yeah."

His shoulders shook with his silent laughter. "I think we're doing just fine. I'm enjoying spending time with you. I won't lie; it's not easy, but I didn't expect it to be."

"I am too. We really don't know too much about our adult selves, so it's been nice to get to know you better." Although I didn't see why we couldn't get to know each other intimately at the same time, who was I to argue?

ELEVEN

"GIRL!" Todd shouted as he came barreling out into the backyard where Dana and I were laying out in the sun.

"Hi to you, too, Todd," Dana quipped.

Todd stopped and put down his phone that he'd been waving in the air. "Oh, hey, Dana, hope you're wearing sunscreen today." He turned away and then looked back at her. "Why are you here so early? Don't you usually come later for girls' night?"

Dana frowned and sat up. "Nice to see you, too, dick. I took a half-day off so we could spend the afternoon lounging by the pool."

I pushed up onto my elbows. "What were you shouting about?"

"Nothing. It's nothing." He was suddenly clamming up, which was not like him at all.

"Oh my God. Spit it out." Dana was just as exasperated as I was.

He gave me an odd look and flicked his eyes to Dana.

She smacked him. "What the fuck, Todd? I can see you. What are you trying to hide from me?"

He sighed dramatically and pulled his phone out of his pocket. "It's nothing really. I was just looking at photos from the *Big Dog's Haven* charity event, and a few popped up that I thought you might like."

Dana snatched the phone out of Todd's hand. "*Oh*, let me see." The smile on her face fell as she scrolled through.

Todd sat down on a chair and huffed out a heavy breath. "See, this is exactly why I didn't want to show you. Ugh!"

I had no clue what was happening. "What am I missing here? Dana, what's wrong?"

She looked up at me with tears in her eyes, and I jumped up immediately to go to her. "Girl, what's the matter?"

She turned the phone around to show me a photo of Foster and me on the dance floor. We were looking up at each other, but other than a few other random people, I wasn't sure why she was so upset, and then it hit me. "Oh my God. I'm so sorry. I never thought about how you'd feel actually seeing the two of us together like that. I promise we were there just as friends and nothing happened. *Nothing*."

She shook her head and dropped it to her hands. "It's not that. If you look through the photos that they took of the two of you, any moron can see the love in his eyes for you. I feel so stupid that I never saw it." She stared at me and smiled through her tears. "You're my best friend, Kam, and if *any other* man would've looked at you that way, I would've told you to get down on one knee and propose. How was I so blind that I missed it?"

"What are you yammering on about? Nothing is going on between us. I mean before there was, but we had this love-hate vibe that no one would've been able to see through. Right now, we're trying out this whole friend thing, and we even talked about it last night. It's kind of nice getting to know him without any of the expectations of dating or…" I decided to leave the sexual aspects out of that sentence. "Give me the damn phone." I snatched it out of Dana's hand and scrolled back through.

I tried not to give away any emotion on my face because she was right. Foster looked at me with adoration, and it melted my cold, black heart. After sending myself the link, I closed the phone. "It's nothing. We we're just dancing and having a good time."

Dana was the first to call me on my crap. "You're so full of shit. How can you not see that?"

"Why do you think I came in here shouting? I hate to agree with Dana, but no way you can be that blind bitch. That boy has it *bad*."

"You guys are ridiculous. Foster's the one who said we should be friends and seems to remind me of it at every opportunity."

Todd looked like he wanted to pull out his hair. Not that he'd ever mess it up like that. "I should slap your lying ass because, in those pictures, it's clear as day that *you* look at him the same way."

"Fuck off." I went back to my lounger. "Go make yourself useful, Todd, and fix us some drinks." I shooed him away, hoping that he'd drop it.

He stood and looked down at me. "Someone's in denial, but I'll make you the drinks because I think you might need them."

The moment the door closed behind him, Dana started again, but this time her voice was serious. "Kam, I'm not trying to pester you, but Todd's right. And you know how hard it is for those words to come out of my mouth. If you have feelings for Foster, what's the problem?"

Reluctantly I pulled up onto my elbows again and looked over at her. "I don't know." That was the God's honest truth.

"You might want to figure that out."

"You don't think I know that? It's not that simple, though. I have a kid to think about. I wasn't even ready to date, and then out of nowhere, Foster pops up. It just happened and not how it should have. But honestly, I'm not sure I would've given him a chance otherwise, so I can't even say I wish all that mess didn't happen. But Foster made it clear he needed me *all in,* and I'm not sure I'm there."

"How does he make you feel?" Her tone was soft as she spoke.

"Ugh," I smirked. "Are we really going to have this conversation about your *brother*?"

"Listen, I love you both. He's my flesh and blood, and you've always been like a sister to me. And although that sounds like incest, I want the best for both of you. You need to be honest with yourself, Kam."

"Truthfully? When I'm with him, nothing else matters. It's killing me that we're just friends. He's even amazing with Charlie. I guess I'm just scared." I shrugged, not sure how else to explain it.

"Scared of what?"

"What's with all the hard-ass questions?"

She laughed but waited for me to continue.

"Of things going wrong. When we're together, it's amazing, but I don't want to get hurt. If I'm *all in,* then that affects Charlie too. I don't want her hurt because of my selfishness."

"Hey!" She waited for me to make eye contact. "Being happy is *not* selfish. You don't have a selfish bone in your body, especially when it comes to your daughter. As much as I hate to admit it, my brother is a pretty great guy. He would do anything for you and Charlie even before. He wouldn't ask you for everything if he weren't willing to give you his whole self."

"I've been through a nasty divorce, and I'm not doing

that all over. I won't make that mistake twice, so I'm just being cautious and holding out for a sign, I guess."

Todd chuckled. "Keep waiting, sweetheart, because signs don't punch you in the face, but I might. You just need to look at the small hints dropped here and there. Those are the ones that matter."

I hadn't even heard Todd come outside, but I was grateful for the glass he handed me. I took a big gulp and tried to shut down the conversation. "I'm working through my shit, all right? I just need a little time."

"Well, don't wait too long, or someone might come along and snatch up that sexy piece of man meat." Leave it to Todd to throw that back in my face.

Like that thought hadn't already crossed my mind a million times. "Ugh! You don't think I've already thought of that?" I really didn't want to continue to have this conversation. I knew everything they were saying was true, and it wasn't anything I hadn't previously told myself.

Dana threw up her hands in surrender. "Okay, I won't bring it up again…today."

I smacked her shoulder, playfully. "You're buying drinks tonight just for that."

"Deal! I can't wait to get my dance on." Dana loved to dance, and she was pretty damn good at it, too, me not so much.

I was glad to be done with our little chat and moving on to mindless exchanges. It was already hard enough to deal with on my own. I knew both of them would be there if I needed them, but I just hoped that now I could get my head in check.

The rest of the day went on without any serious conversations about relationships or futures, and for that, I was thankful. By the time the Uber dropped us off at Shenanigans, I was ready to let loose and have a good time.

Drinks were the first order of business for Dana while I grabbed us a table. We didn't waste a minute before we got out on the dance floor. We were the only ones out there, but I didn't care. It felt good to let go and just move to the music without a care in the world. *Wannabe* by the *Spice Girls* came on, and we went crazy just like we did when we were teenagers—Charlie would be mortified.

As soon as our glasses were empty, we took a break. I made sure I was conscious of the fact I was wearing a skirt as I sat down and dropped my new pair of black stilettos to the ground and rubbed the soles of my feet. I wasn't usually one to wear heels—I could barely walk in them—but I had to admit I was doing fairly well dancing in them.

Dana set down my drink and leaned into me. "Don't look now, but Todd just walked in, and he's *not* alone."

Instinctively I started to turn, but Dana gripped my chin to stop me. "What the fuck? I said, *don't* look." She rolled her eyes at me as she rounded the table to sit across from me.

I was just about to ask who it was, but I caught a hint of his cologne. Dana must have noticed the shocked look on my face as my eyes bugged out of my head as she shrugged without a word.

Todd rested his hand on the back of my seat. "Hey, ladies!" He leaned over to kiss my cheek, and I hissed into his ear. "What the fuck, Todd?"

He pulled back with mock innocence written on his face as he clutched his chest. "Why such vulgar language? I thought since we are all *friends,* we could hang for the night." The smile behind his eyes had me wanting to smack him.

Foster stepped to my other side, looking between Todd and me. "I can leave if it's a problem. I told Todd it was girls' night, but he said it would be fine since you always invite him."

Ugh! Now I felt bad. I didn't mean to make Foster uncomfortable. "No, no. It's fine. Have a seat."

He eyed me suspiciously.

I flagged down the server so they could order drinks. "Sit down, Foster."

He sat down beside me as smug Todd plopped down on my other side. I was going to give him an earful later. He knew exactly what he was doing.

The drinks flowed as I tried to let it all go and enjoy our

night. When I really thought about it, I wasn't even sure why I was upset in the first place. I loved spending time with Foster and Todd as well. Having Foster there was just another slap in my face that I was falling for him, and there wasn't anything I could do to stop it—even if I wanted to.

Dana suddenly stood from her seat. "As much as I'm enjoying this engaging conversation, Kam and I come here to get our dance on, and that's what we are going to do. So either join us or chat amongst yourselves." She reached out her hand for me to take and pulled me behind her without looking back.

I couldn't help but laugh at my best friend. She was right; it was *girls' night* regardless of whether there were guys with us, and they could either join in the festivities or do their own thing.

It didn't take long for them to make their way out to the dance floor. Todd loved to strut his stuff for all to see, and I knew from spending more time with Foster that he had a few of his own moves. We welcomed them into our circle and shook our asses like they weren't even there.

Foster kept his distance. But after Todd went back to the table and a man came up to dance with Dana, he took the in and slowly moved closer to me. I tried to ignore him as best I could. As much as I wanted his hands all over me, I didn't think it was appropriate to do so in front of his sister. Dana turned around and got a little closer to her partner, who was more of a Greek god than a man.

Foster stayed behind me as he wrapped me in his arms and began grinding against my ass. I could feel his length as he rubbed up against me. He trailed a hand down my side and down to the hem of my skirt. The feel of his breath at my ear had goose bumps forming. "Please tell me there are panties under this skirt." His voice sounded strained.

I smirked, knowing I had the upper hand for once. Reaching my hand up, I gripped the back of his neck as I ground back into Foster's thickening cock. "Why does it matter, Mr. Montgomery?"

He groaned in my ear. "You know what…don't answer that. I don't want to know."

I kept my expression innocent as I turned around to face him. "Is there a problem, Foster?" I kept dancing, but he seemed to be having trouble concentrating.

He dropped his forehead to mine and closed his eyes as he took a deep breath. "You're killing me, Poodle."

The nickname caused me to snicker. "I'm not sure what I'm doing, but as my friend, what I'm wearing under my skirt shouldn't really concern you. I bet Todd and Dana wouldn't ask me, although they might question my sanity for going out in this skirt without any panties—that's neither here nor there."

He pulled back slightly. "You and your smart mouth." His eyes flicked between my eyes and my lips, and then before I had a second to think, he gripped the back of my neck and crashed his lips to mine. Instinctively my hands wrapped around him, and the world around us ceased to exist. I had to talk myself out of climbing him like a monkey on a tree right in the middle of Shenanigans. He pulled back before I was ready, and a whimper escaped my throat.

He looked down at me with hooded eyes. "I'm not even sorry." His voice was a whisper.

My inner middle-schooler was jumping for joy, but I tamped her down before responding, "Good." It was all I could muster without asking him to come home with me, and I couldn't take it if he said no.

The smile that crossed his lips revealed that dimple I loved so much. I reached up and ran my finger down his cheek. He opened his mouth to say something, but he must've decided against it and asked me if I wanted a drink instead.

Although I was curious about what was going through his head, I just nodded and followed him back to the table, where we found Todd holding his glass with a self-satisfied smirk on his face. I wasn't sure if I wanted to hug him or smack the shit out of him. I'd decide tomorrow.

Todd leaned into Foster and nudged him. "How's it make you feel that there's a schmexy-ass man all up on your sister?"

"Well, I wouldn't call him *schmexy* as you so

eloquently put it, and I wasn't paying much attention to it, but thank you so much for turning my attention in their direction. I really appreciate that. You're becoming such a great friend."

Clearly, Foster's sarcasm was lost on Todd as he sat up taller and smacked him on the shoulder as guys do. "Any time, buddy."

I bit my tongue. Guys can be so dumb, and there really was no purpose in pointing it out since it wouldn't change anything. It's just part of their genetic makeup.

Dana walked over as her guy went to the bar. I stood up and pulled her toward the restroom.

Finally, in the quiet of the restroom, I could ask, "I want some answers. Who was that hottie?"

She smiled. "Right? His name is Cole. I have actually met him before, a friend of a friend. Hey, you don't mind, if he asks, if I go home with him, do you?"

"You're such a whore! Of course, I don't mind. Get it, girl!" I would never cause a cliterference.

"Thanks. Either way, I'll be there in the morning so we can go for breakfast."

We finished our lady business and headed back out. Dana went to find Cole at the bar, and I went back to the table. I wanted to tell Dana about the kiss, but I didn't know what the protocol was here when the guy you're crushing on is your best friend's brother. I would need to talk to her about this and see how she wanted me to deal with it going forward.

Todd stood suddenly—snapping me out of my thoughts—and slipped his phone into his pocket. "So, I'm going to head out." He fake yawned dramatically, even going so far as to stretch his hands high above his head. "Maybe I'll see you tomorrow if I don't come up with anything better to do. Maybe a poolside lounge day?" Todd said, trying to sound nonchalant, but it was no use trying to hide anything. He was an open book to me.

I knew he wouldn't spill right now, so I didn't bother pushing. "I'll be around, but if you arrive before eleven without coffee, you're in big shit."

We both laughed, but he was clearly dying to get out of there.

I nodded toward Dana, who was playing tonsil hockey with Cole. She definitely wouldn't be back that early. "I don't think Dana will need one."

"I think you're right." He reached his hand out for Foster to shake, and they said their goodbyes before Todd came around my side.

I stood and leaned over to give him a one-armed hug, and I felt a hand wander up my skirt as I did so. *Fucking men.* I rolled my eyes internally. "I'll be expecting that coffee tomorrow," I said before he walked away. I slapped Foster's hand away from my ass. "Really? You couldn't hold back while I hugged him goodbye?"

He blinked innocently but then grinned. "Absolutely not, if you have that fine ass sticking out in front of me, in my eyes, that's an open invitation. It's too tempting. Plus, I know you aren't wearing panties under that skirt of yours." His words had my mind racing with all the things I wanted to do to him, and if I were anywhere but here, I would be riding him until the sun came up.

I leaned in and kissed him softly. "Come home with me."

His eyes went wide, and I instantly wanted to take my words back, but it was too late. I moved back in my seat and swallowed hard. "Sorry, just forget I said anything."

"Fat chance of that. Is that the alcohol talking?"

I whipped my head up to look at him. "Why would you think that?"

"I just needed to ask to be sure."

The alcohol made me brazen, but I didn't need it to want Foster at all. "I don't know how you do this to me, but you cause me to lose my bloody mind when you touch me—alcohol or not."

He smiled at me. "Good answer."

A few minutes after Todd had left, Dana came to stand in front of me on the table. "Do you mind—"

I cut her off. "No, I don't mind. Have fun, girl. You're still coming for brunch, though, right? Todd also mentioned poolside lounge day again."

She squealed and kissed me on the forehead. "I'll totally be there. My pale-white ass could use some more sun." She stopped and looked at Foster. "Umm…have a good night?"

Foster shook his head. "You aren't seriously going home with a stranger?"

Dana pursed her lips and propped her hand on her hip. "Do you think I'm crazy? I know him. Well, not *well*, but I've met him before. He's a friend of a friend, so chill out." She kissed his cheek. "Love you."

"Love you too."

We sat there and watched as Dana and Cole left the bar. Thank God for the music because the silence would've been awkward.

He turned to me and rested his arms on the table. "So…"

I mimicked his position. "So…"

"You want to get out of here?"

I stood instantly and grabbed my purse. Foster's face lit up, and he followed suit.

The drive to my place was silent other than the soft sounds of country music on the radio. When we pulled into my driveway, Foster threw the truck in park and turned to me.

"I was thinking," his eyes were sad, and I wasn't sure that I wanted to hear what he had to say, "as much as I am dying to come in, I'm not sure it's a good idea."

I swallowed hard. "Okay…"

He was probably right, but I wanted him. "It's taking every bit of strength not to take you right now, but I don't think it'll solve anything. Things are going great, and don't get me wrong, I would love to take things to the next level, but I know you still need time."

"I understand. I guess one of us has to be the grown-up here." The back of my throat stung as I held back tears that I hadn't expected to surface. I turned away and opened my door. "Thanks for the ride."

Foster grabbed my arm to pull me back to him. His hands palmed my face as he kissed me softly. "Goodnight, Kam." He breathed against my lips.

INCESSANT BANGING WOKE me from an amazing dream. The clock on my wall told me it was just passed ten. "Who the fuck is up this early?" I practically fell in my attempt to get out of bed. I'd helped myself to a few more drinks after Foster had turned me down last night and my head wasn't happy. I cleared the sleep from my eyes and threw on a pair of sweats to go see who I needed to kill.

To my surprise, Foster stood on the other side of the door.

"Good morning, beautiful. Did I wake you?" His dimple appeared, and the anger I felt a moment ago vanished, but I wasn't letting him off that easy.

"Yes, of course, you did. Do you have any idea what time it is and how much alcohol I consumed last night?"

He chuckled. "You didn't drink that much. I was there, remember?"

I turned to walk back inside without inviting him in. "Yeah, well, I had a few more after you dropped me off. And I can't believe you showed up without Starbucks. That's an unwritten rule, you know?"

"I knew Todd would be coming with it shortly. Anyway, I got you something." He handed me a pink gift box with a large white bow on it.

It was light in my hands as I took it from him. "Is this the *I'm sorry for not boning you last night* gift?" I was still a little butt-hurt over that, and I wasn't planning on getting over it anytime soon.

"No. Although I wanted to come in, I'm not sorry that I didn't. I want to do things right."

I plopped down on the sofa without coffee, praying that Todd would be here soon. "Fair enough."

"I'm sort of regretting this gift now. I thought it was a good idea at the time." He went to swipe it from me, but I pulled it away.

"Fuck no. Now I really need to see it." I ripped the bow off before he could say another word.

He groaned but just sat there waiting. Opening the top of the box, I was confused because there was a pile of lace, silk, and cotton amongst the tissue paper inside. I looked up at him with a furrowed brow, and he just shrugged. I pulled one out and laughed—a full-on belly clutching cackle. "Really, Foster?"

He opened his mouth, but nothing came out. I could barely speak through my hysterics. *What was he thinking?*

"What made you think this would be a good gift for me?" He knew I didn't wear panties, so I wasn't sure where his mind was at.

Suddenly his face went red, and he looked shy. "It's more of a gift for me."

"Umm…how?"

"Last night you went out to a bar in a sexy-as-fuck skirt wearing *no panties*. All I could think about is one false step and everyone in the bar would see that pussy of yours, and I was *not* okay with that."

I almost told him to mind his own damn business, but there was something about his demeanor that had me keeping quiet.

"I know you aren't *mine*, but I couldn't help myself. *Fuck*." He gripped the back of his neck in frustration. "This all played out differently in my head."

On the one hand, his gift was controlling, but on the other, it was a man's weird way of showing that I was his, even though *technically* I wasn't.

I pulled a handful of them out. He must have bought forty pairs. "I honestly haven't worn these things in years. I think one pair would've gotten your point across." Then I noticed the tags and started doing the math in my head. *"Holy shit!* How much did you spend?"

"That's irrelevant. Can you promise me that if you go out in a skirt or a dress, you'll wear a pair?"

"I can't promise that since remembering to wear them would be the issue, but I can *try*. Although it's really none of your business." I raised a brow, daring him to challenge me on this.

"Touché."

The front door opened, and Todd strutted into the living room. This was going to be good. "Girl...." He drew out the word as he always did when he had juicy gossip. He noticed Foster, and his face soured. "Why do you always have *people* here? Every time I want to gush too." His eyes rolled as he came to stand beside me.

His hand reached into the box and hung a pair of panties from his finger. "Turning over a new leaf here, Kam?" He snickered. "Finally going to stop going commando?"

"Fuck, no, these things are so uncomfortable." I snatched the pair from Todd and covered the box back up before putting it on the floor. "Foster here thinks I should wear them when I wear a skirt."

Todd gave him a high five, which was quite out of character for him. "Thank you. I've been telling her for years that she can't go out all free-range. It's one thing with pants or a long, fitted dress but short skirts. *Hell, no!*"

"Fuck you both." I tried to snatch my coffee from him, but he moved it out of reach.

Dana walked in just at the right moment to pluck it from the tray and hand it to me.

"Thank you. At least I have one friend I can count on." I kissed her cheek when she sat down beside me.

She smirked and looked between Foster and me. "Did he?"

Todd answered for me. "Nope, he brought Kam a present." He nodded his head toward the box.

Did he really have to bring attention to that? "Oh. My. God." I blew out a loud breath.

"Aw, what did my big oaf of a brother get you?"

"Nothing." I pulled my legs up under me on the couch and sipped my coffee. "So, what's the plan for today?"

"Nice try." Dana scooped up the box and opened it. She burst out laughing. "Why even bother?" She looked up at Foster. "Do you even know her?"

"Nope." The sound of the *P* popping drew attention to his irritation. "Not at all."

"Can we please drop it?" I turned to Todd with pleading eyes, but he either didn't understand or didn't give a shit.

"He bought them, so Kamryn here wasn't at risk for showing her lady bits to anyone but him."

I hopped up off the couch. "That's it, conversation over." Looking at Foster, I tried to apologize for my friends. "Want to help me get something to eat?"

He didn't answer but came with me as we left the

snickering middle-schoolers in the other room to calm their laughter.

I opened the refrigerator and grabbed some eggs. "Sorry about that. They can be a little too much sometimes."

"It's cool. My sister can be a bitch. I also didn't think they'd be here until eleven."

"Me either. They probably both want to gossip about their nights. Dana won't do that with you obviously, and Todd got sidetracked by the panties."

Thank God by the time we ate and went back to the other room, they'd settled down a bit. Todd was finally able to focus and gush about Jeff—AKA man bun—and all the juicy details. Foster stayed for a little bit but had to get going to a meeting.

TWELVE

"WE'RE GOING TO FUCKING DIE." Todd gripped the oh-shit handle above his window with his eyes held shut as he sat in the passenger seat of my car.

"Language! There are virgin ears here." Charlie heard it all the time, but I couldn't help but bother him. "And we aren't going to die. I drive every day, and we're just fine. Right, Charlie?"

She didn't even budge since she was on her phone with her AirPods in her ears.

I turned the corner, and Todd moved his other hand up to hold onto the handle. "Oh, Jesus."

"Why didn't you get someone else to drive you if you were going to be like this. You're such a drama queen."

We were headed to Dana's birthday party at her parents' place. Todd had hurt his foot when he went out dancing last night and couldn't drive himself.

"I tried. I'd invited Jeff to come, but he had to work. I even asked Foster, but he couldn't take me since his mom had him helping set up early this morning. You were the last resort. I almost canceled but knew Dana would be pissed." He still hadn't opened his eyes.

"Wow! So I was your last resort? Nice. I'll remember that the next time you need something. And if you'd open your eyes, it wouldn't be so bad. You can't see when I am going to turn or anything, so it all feels scary."

Todd didn't budge, but I could see the muscles straining in his arms as he gripped harder.

I smacked him in the chest. "Just open your damn eyes and stop being sexist. Not all women are bad drivers."

He finally turned to look at me. "No, they're not. You're right about that. *You* are a bad driver."

I shook my head and ignored him. I wasn't a bad driver. I had never even been in an accident before, so I tried to brush it off and turned up the music.

Todd went back to closed eyes and clutching the handle as I just sang and danced in my seat while I drove us to the party. I was looking forward to seeing Dana's family and some old friends, and he wasn't going to ruin that for me.

Charlie snickered from the back seat. "Uncle Todd, why are you holding on like that?"

"Oh, sweetie, Todd here is what we call an attention seeker who's blowing things out of proportion. We don't want to follow in his footsteps. He thinks I'm going to kill him with my so-called crazy driving." I rolled my eyes at her in the rearview mirror, causing her giggles to kick up a notch.

"I'm not going to dignify either one of you with a response." Todd blew out an exasperated sigh.

Charlie put her AirPods back in; she'd seemingly had enough of our conversation.

The rest of the trip was fairly silent other than the sporadic groans and inhalations from Todd. By the time we pulled into the driveway, I was ready to push Todd out of the car—while we were still moving.

Dana greeted us in the driveway, and Todd dramatically ran into her arms. "I cannot go home with that woman."

"Oh my God, Todd. Are you still going on? You can seriously walk the fuck home."

He'd taken this way too far. I honestly wasn't at all a bad driver, so he was going overboard.

I gave Dana a quick hug before Charlie and I went around back to say hello to everyone. I was over Todd at that point and needed to calm down before I slapped the shit out of him in the middle of the party. Dana's parents came over immediately and engulfed the two of us. I hadn't seen them in a few months, so it was good to catch up. We made our rounds—well, Charlie followed and didn't say much—and then we took a seat under the shade. I hadn't put on sunscreen and didn't want to turn into a lobster today.

Dana came to us with Todd in tow. If he said one

more thing, I would probably snap, and the scowl I gave him perhaps told him not to fuck with me because he didn't say another word about my driving.

I stood up to go to the restroom. "I'll be right back. Charlie, stay here."

Her nod was imperceptible, and she didn't even look up. Damn kids.

As I walked inside through the back door, I secretly hoped to run into Foster since I hadn't seen him yet. No luck on the way to the bathroom, but on the way out, I heard his voice. I wandered closer to the kitchen and stopped in my tracks as I heard Mrs. Montgomery's voice.

"She's a sweet girl. I told her mother that I would talk to you about setting up a blind date. I'm sure you would like her, sweetie."

I swallowed hard, waiting for his response.

"I'm not interested in a blind date set up by my *mother*." He sounded amused.

She sighed. "You're just as stubborn as your father. Let me grab my phone and show you a photo. She's a very pretty blonde. I know you two would hit it off."

"Mom…" He almost whined. "Listen, I'm already seeing someone."

"You are?" Her voice shrieked as she expressed her excitement.

"Yes, it's really new, and I didn't want to tell anyone until it was more serious."

My stomach dropped, and tears stung the back of my eyes.

"Oh, sweetie, that's so great. I can't wait to meet her. What's her name? What's she like?"

My throat burned as I tried to hold back the tears. I backed up, needing to get back to the bathroom quickly. The console table behind me squeaked as my foot hit it; I ran to the bathroom before Foster or his mother could come out and catch me eavesdropping.

The moment the bathroom door shut, I ran the water, splashing my face to calm myself. I looked up at myself in the mirror. I couldn't break down—I wouldn't.

What did you think would happen, stupid?

Did I really think he was going to wait around? I'd been dragging my feet for the past few weeks. I even told myself numerous times that someone was going to come and snatch him up.

Ugh.

I splashed my face one more time and dried it off with a hand towel. Today was about Dana; I could have a meltdown later.

The words to Kesha's "Woman" played in my head like a soundtrack. *I got this.*

Gripping the door handle, I took a deep breath and turned the knob. I walked out and started down the hall without looking where I was going and slammed into a hard chest. I stumbled backward, but large hands held me up and pulled me back in. "You should really watch where you're going there, Poodle." Foster sounded amused, but I didn't crack a smile.

I kept my eyes down and hands to myself. "Sorry, I didn't see you."

He reached for my chin, forcing me to look up at him. "Everything okay, Kam?"

"Yeah. I'm just heading back outside." I tried to pull away and move around him. "Excuse me."

"Kam." Concern filled his voice.

"Foster," his mother called from down the hall. "Sweetie, you should've invited your girlfriend today. It would've been a great time to meet her."

I peered around Foster at Mrs. Montgomery.

"Oh, sorry, Kam, I didn't see you there. Did you hear that my baby has a girlfriend?"

I looked up at Foster with a sad smile. "No, ma'am, I didn't, but that's great, Foster. Congrats." I took that opportunity to escape.

Foster tried to stop me, but I pulled my arm free. "Kam, wait."

I ignored his panicked voice and smiled as I passed his mother.

"Fuck," I heard him whisper under his breath.

"Don't speak like that, Foster," she scolded.

"Not now, Mom."

I heard his loud footsteps as he tried to catch up with me, but I was already outside by the time he did.

"Kam, please. Let me explain."

Now that we were in the safety of other company, I plastered on a sweet smile and turned around. "I'm not sure what you need to explain, Foster. You don't owe me anything. You aren't *mine*." The words I spat stung me more than him, but I needed to protect myself here.

"Really? That's how you want to play this?"

I stepped toward him, not wanting to make a scene. "I'm not playing Foster. I'm really pleased that you've found someone. You deserve to be happy."

He ran his hand through his hair and gripped the back of his neck. He looked back up at me and then turned to look over where Charlie sat with some other kids around her age. He seemed to be struggling with what to say but then finally conceded. "Fine. Thanks, Kam." And with that, he walked away.

Dana took off after him and pulled at his arm for him to stop. Her hands were flailing like a complete lunatic as she looked to be cussing him out. I smiled inside that my best friend was on my side—even against her brother. She stopped after a few minutes and then walked back over to us with a smirk on her face.

Todd asked before I could. "What is that look on your face for?"

"Nothing. Just my brother's a dumbass."

She could say that again. I wish I hadn't driven because I could really use a drink or ten. I tried my best to think about anything but Foster and the fact that he was seeing someone else, but it was nearly impossible. I kept catching myself watching him every few seconds. He was sitting over near Charlie and the younger kids, and I couldn't help but notice that when he looked at her, affection glowed in his eyes. He looked at her like—well, like I did. Right then, the final piece to the puzzle clicked into place. I'd fallen for Foster a long time ago, but at that moment, I fell past the point of no return. No more of this friend bull shit. I was all in, and I was going to prove it. Girlfriend or not, I didn't give a shit.

Charlie looked up at me, and I signaled for her to come with me. I needed to have a chat with her. She followed me around the side of the house where I sat her down and word vomited everything—well, not *every*thing. I didn't need her permission, but we were a team, and I felt like I owed it to her.

She looked up at me with a big grin on her face. "You really like him, huh?"

"Yeah, I guess I kind of do."

She kissed my cheek sweetly. "Then get him. You deserve to be happy." Sometimes she was much wiser than her years.

"Are you sure? This could have a huge impact on our lives as we know it—that is if he doesn't turn me down."

She rolled her eyes. "Mom, even I can see that he likes you. I think you're good, and yes, I'm cool with everything."

I hugged my baby girl tightly before pulling back and holding her at arm's length. "So you might think I'm a little crazy for what I'm about to do. Please don't let it change how you see me."

"You *are* crazy, and it's part of why I love you."

"I love you too." I kissed her on the forehead and went back to the party. I think at that moment was when I lost touch with reality completely and went on auto-pilot. All of a sudden, I was standing on a picnic table in my best friend's parents' backyard in front of probably fifty people, most of whom were staring at me. The yard had suddenly grown silent, and my stomach was feeling queasy. I searched the crowd for the only set of eyes I needed to see. Charlie was standing beside him with a huge smirk on her face as she nudged him and nodded in my direction.

He looked up at me and cocked a brow—clearly wondering what this crazy bitch was doing standing on a picnic table. I took a deep breath and smiled at him, which he reciprocated, and that was enough for me to get on with it.

"Foster," I felt like I was going to barf all over, "I—"

He slowly walked toward me with Charlie beside him. He stopped when he stood in front of me.

I could breathe a little easier knowing that they were both right there, and I didn't have to speak so loud. "I love you. I don't know what took me so long to realize it, but I'm head-over-heels in love with you. I know this isn't the greatest timing seeing that you have a girlfriend now, but I needed you to know how serious I am."

"*We* are," Charlie said as she looked up at Foster with a smile so big.

Foster looked between Charlie and me with a huge smile on his face—that damn dimple.

"Yes, *we* are…" I took a deep breath, trying to hold the waterworks at bay, but it was no use. A tear slipped free, and I whispered, "All in."

"Yeah?" His voice was barely a whisper as he looked down at Charlie. "You all in, too, kiddo?"

She shrugged but nodded. "Sure. Whatever that means."

Foster shook his head as he chuckled. "Good enough." He hopped up onto the picnic table with me and held my face in the palms of his hands. "I hope you know that I'm never letting you go. All in means all in."

"I'll be holding you to that."

"I love you, Poodle." He leaned in and kissed me breathless. Everyone clapped and cheered around us, but they quickly became background noise.

When we finally came up for air, he pulled me into his side as we looked out over everyone standing there, witnessing our confessions of love. "So who's coming to the wedding?" he shouted, and I nearly choked at the thought of a big wedding again.

Everyone's chatter and good spirits weren't helping. A wedding was very stressful.

I got up on my tiptoes to whisper in his ear, "Can we just go to Vegas or some shit, even the beach?"

"Whatever you want, baby."

He stepped down off the picnic table and lifted me down, keeping me close by. Charlie still stood there, but she was focused on her phone and not paying us one bit of attention.

Foster's family quickly circled around. Dana pushed her way through them. "Oh. Em. Gee. I can't believe you just got up on a table in front of all these people and did that!" She smacked her brother. "You have no idea how much she hates public speaking. She must really love you—oh, and you hurt her, and you're dead to me. This is my chance to have a sister, and she's already my best friend. How cool is that?" She pulled me in for a hug before letting others have a turn.

His mom stepped up and smacked him too. "Young man. I love Kamryn, but you told me just today that you had started seeing someone. Cheating is *not* tolerated in this house."

Foster clutched his stomach as he laughed. "I was talking about Kamryn. She's been the one for me for a while now; I was just waiting on her to catch up to where I was at."

I beamed up at him. He was so confident that we were meant to be that he had waited. I was truly grateful there was no other woman—I really didn't want to have to kick someone's ass.

"Oh, thank God." She hugged us both. "I'm happy

for you two. This is so exciting. I can't wait to plan a wedding," she shrieked.

Foster must've felt me stiffen at his side as he squeezed me tightly. "Mama, how about a quiet beach wedding with a small family reception?"

Her face fell a little, but she nodded. "Sounds beautiful."

"Don't worry. You can plan a huge wedding for me." Dana never talked about a wedding or marriage ever, so that was a little surprising.

Mrs. Montgomery turned to her with pursed lips. "Since when are you getting married?"

"Ugh!" The two of them got into a deep discussion, and we slowly crept away.

We took a seat, and I leaned into his side.

He pulled an AirPod out of Charlie's ear. "So who's house are we going to live in?"

Charlie just shrugged like it was nothing.

"Charlie, do you like animals?" he asked.

That got her attention. "I love them."

"So I know your mom just admitted that she loves me, but I've pretty much been in love with her since I was a kid. We talked once about living on a farm and adopting a bunch of animals. What do you think?"

I went to interject, thinking this was way too much for her in one day, but she beamed at him and just responded with, "Hell, yes!"

I didn't correct her language since I was in complete shock at her response.

"Woah. Are you two crazy? This is a little too fast, and Charlie, sweetie, you would most likely have to change schools."

She looked up in thought. "That's okay. Most of my friends are dance friends—wait, I wouldn't have to change dance studios, right?"

"No, but school, starting over is hard at your age." I couldn't even believe we were having this conversation. I knew Charlie was resilient, but this seemed like overload for any child.

"Would I get to pick these animals? Because if I could, then I'm in. I want lots of animals. Could I get a trampoline too?"

Foster laughed, and I sat there, dumbfounded.

"This is just too much." I shook my head.

Foster leaned down and kissed the top of my head. "This is what all in is, baby. We're doing this."

THIRTEEN

FOSTER AGREED to let me take some time to ease into the *all-in* aspect of our relationship. He spent most nights at our house over the next few months but had been really good about not bringing up the future.

Charlie, on the other hand, was not so good at it. She was excited about the prospect of living on a farm and wanting a bazillion animals. I was glad that she was still on board after all this time, and it wasn't just a decision she was making on a whim.

"I thought I should sell my house. I'm rarely there, so it's a waste." He lifted his finger to silence me. "I'm not trying to pressure you, so if you're not ready, I'm okay with that too."

"I wasn't going to say that. I think that's a good plan, and I think we should revisit the farm idea. When I think about looking for a house, I cringe because it's so hard to find something we can all agree on but I think I'm ready."

His eyes went wide, and he smiled. "Yeah?"

"Yeah."

"Oh, baby, I'm so excited." He looked over at Charlie. "It's time."

I wasn't sure what they meant. "Time for what?"

Charlie took off out of the room.

"You'll see," he said without elaborating.

The two of them were conspiring against me. Great. I loved that they were getting along, but ganging up on me was unacceptable.

Charlie ran back into the room, and they turned toward each other, whispering about something I couldn't quite hear. They turned to me, and both got down on one knee. Charlie opened a ring box while Foster took my left hand.

"Kamryn, I've been dying—" he turned to Charlie— "well, *we've* been dying to ask you this for months now."

Charlie smiled. "We love you and can't wait to be a family."

"Poodle, will you marry me?"

My free hand flew to my open mouth. I knew he was serious about us, but I wasn't expecting this.

Charlie cleared her throat obnoxiously and nudged Foster. "Maybe she doesn't like ya. Sorry about your luck, buddy, I tried."

We all burst out laughing. "You're such a brat." I dropped to my knees in front of him and brought my mouth close to his. "Yes," I whispered against his lips. "Yes."

Foster took the two of us in a bear hug, and we all fell to the ground. "She said, yes!"

It all felt surreal as I lay in the arms of my now fiancé with my daughter, who was giggling away. I knew that everything would be all right and that this was how things were meant to be.

"OH MY GOD, Todd, slow down. You're going to kill us." I gripped the door handle and center console of Todd's car dramatically as Todd turned a corner.

Charlie gripped the back of Todd's seat. "Yeah, Uncle Todd, are you crazy? We're all going to die before the wedding. How tragic would that be?"

We'd been playing this game the whole way to the beach, and he was getting extremely annoyed. But it was my wedding day, and I figured I would do whatever I wanted to.

"Okay, guys, I get it. You've proven your point. Now shut your pie holes." He was smirking still, so at least we hadn't pushed him over the edge.

Dana leaned forward. "Honestly, Todd, did you expect anything less when you offered to drive the three of us?"

"I guess not. I should've known better." He turned up the radio—even though he wasn't a fan of Justin Bieber—and we all sang along.

Today was my wedding day, and I couldn't have been more excited about it. Todd had been asked by Foster to be one of his groomsmen, and although I really wanted Todd standing behind me, I was glad he and Foster had formed a friendship. So I made Todd agree to hang out all morning until the wedding when he went over to the guy's side. I couldn't wait to say our vows and get on with the rest of our lives together. It was weird because although I'd been married before and that relationship had failed miserably, I had no fears or second thoughts about this one. I knew beyond a shadow of a doubt that Foster was the man I'd grow old with.

We came to a stop, and tears stung my eyes as I looked out over the water. I saw the arbor set up on the beach, and it looked beautiful. I'd basically let the women in my life control every aspect of the ceremony. My only conditions were lilies, close friends and family only, and on the beach. Everything else was fair game, and they didn't disappoint. My mom, Foster's mom, Dana, and even Charlie all had a hand in every detail, and that made it all the more special.

I turned around to face them. "It's perfect, you guys. Thank you."

They both kissed my cheek.

"What am I chopped liver?" Todd seemed offended. "I helped too. You think these women could ever pull off something that picturesque without me?" He huffed in exasperation as he rolled his eyes.

"Aw. Thank you, Toddey Woddey." I pinched his cheek, and he pulled away.

"Ugh! I hate when you call me that." He took a few deep breaths and then parked the car in front of the small hall where we'd be having the reception. "Now get out. Let's get you hitched."

I jumped out of my car, holding the train of my dress to avoid stepping on it. I'd chosen a long, fitted, simple gown. I wasn't a fancy person, so it fit my style perfectly.

We all relaxed in the room they'd designated as my dressing room and had a glass of champagne. I even allowed Charlie to have a small glass. My mom and Mrs. Montgomery joined us as well. It was nice to sit around with all the women—and Todd—I loved and share stories of our lives before the big moment.

It felt like I was waiting forever, so the moment my dad knocked on the door, I jumped out of my seat. He couldn't have come at a better time as I was starting to get antsy. I was dying to see my groom.

I clapped my hands together in excitement. "Let's do this, ladies—" I turned to my dad and then Todd and smiled—"and gents." I stopped just before exiting the room to face them. "Any last words of wisdom from any of you?"

They all shook their heads, but Charlie had

something to say as per usual. "Don't trip on your way down the aisle."

Everyone chuckled at my little brat. "Thanks, Charlie, so much wisdom in those words. I guess since you're the junior maid of honor, you better be sure to hold the train properly, and I should be okay. If I trip, you'll be to blame."

"Oh, wow, thanks, Mom. Pressure much?"

I kissed her forehead, and we headed out the door. My body was vibrating with anticipation.

The sun was just starting to set as we stepped out into the ocean air. Flower petals covered the sand, pointing me in the direction of the man I was about to marry. I linked arms with my dad, and the music started as soon as we rounded the corner, alerting everyone it was time to stand. My eyes went straight to Foster standing under the arbor, and everyone else became a blur.

His smile was huge—revealing that dimple I loved so much—and his eyes never left mine. My pace picked up slightly. I couldn't wait any longer. When my dad finally passed my hand to Foster, I could breathe again. He mouthed *I love you,* and I did the same.

I wasn't much for public speaking, so I'd begged Foster to nix the idea of writing our own vows—repeating after the priest was just about all I could take. I knew how he felt about me, and he knew how I felt about him, and that was all that mattered. The ceremony felt like it took a lifetime for them to say, *'you may kiss the bride,'* but it was worth the wait—the kiss was magical like something movies were made of.

Foster and I danced back up the aisle with our hands raised high.

"Who's ready to party?" Foster said, and everyone cheered.

I was looking forward to a night of dancing and drinks. Foster pulled me to the front entrance instead of to the hall and stopped.

"I'm coming," Charlie shouted from behind us. I turned to find a cheeky grin on her face.

I could just imagine what they were up to. "What is going on? You two are always keeping me out of the loop."

"Oh. Em. Gee. Mom, you're going to love this." She pushed open the door and turned back to us. "What are you waiting for?"

I stopped and pulled back slightly on Foster before he was able to get me through the door. "Wait. We can't leave our wedding."

"Yes, you can, Mom. Everyone already knows that you'll be back soon. Let's go!" She was bouncing on the balls of her feet.

"Someone's impatient." Foster pulled a piece of fabric out of his pocket. "Blindfold first." He covered my eyes with the fabric and guided me to his truck. I didn't question him; I trusted him explicitly.

He started the engine, and we were off—in what direction I couldn't tell, but I was excited either way.

"Eeek! Mom, wait until you see your surprise."

I loved how excited Charlie was. It made this all the more special no matter what it was. "Can I get a hint?"

"Can we, Foster?" Charlie sounded like she was five years old all over again.

He chuckled. "Hmm. Can you think of one that won't give it away?"

"Nope. She can wait." She was such a little shit.

"Thanks, kiddo. Way to look out for me."

"Sorry, Mom, it won't be long, and then you can see."

She was right. What felt like minutes later, we pulled to a stop. Foster's door opened, and he came around and opened mine and helped me out, and then I heard Charlie clambering out of the back.

They each took one of my hands and led me to where I needed to go and then took off the blindfold. My eyes had to adjust to the light, but then I looked around at grass—lots and lots of grass.

"Surprise!" Charlie's voice came from beside me.

I wasn't sure what I was looking at, so I just looked around. "I'm not sure what I'm looking at here."

Charlie spun me around and said, "Our new house."

Now that I was facing the other direction, I saw the beautiful wraparound porch, large pillars, and floor-to-ceiling windows. It was…perfect. I turned to Foster. "Did you buy this?"

"Technically, no. I haven't signed the final paperwork. I felt it was a decision we should make together. Clearly, Charlie's already approved, but I wanted you to see it too."

"About that. When did you two get the time to come check this place out without my knowing?" I was really glad they'd been spending time together but was curious as well.

"We'll never reveal our secret." Foster unlocked the front door. "Are you ready to see inside?"

"Hell yeah, I can't wait."

Charlie pushed passed us. "Come see my room first, Mom. Wait until you see how pretty it is."

I looked over at Foster and cocked a brow. He just shrugged and took my hand as we climbed the winding staircase after Charlie. I took in the details around me as we walked up the stairs. The weathered-grey wood floors and beautifully detailed moldings were stunning. Every element was impeccable. I couldn't wait to see the kitchen.

Charlie hollered for us to hurry from down the hall. Foster led the way. We walked in and found her standing there, grinning from ear to ear. The room was in the corner of the house with windows galore.

"Did you see the chandelier? It's so pretty." She came and grabbed my hand to pull me around the corner. "You aren't even ready for this, but I'll show you anyway. She opened the door and gestured for me to enter like Vanna White.

The door led to a huge walk-in closet that was to die for. It was decked out with wall-to-wall organizers, a large mirror, and a built-in round ottoman in the center.

"Can you believe it, Mom? Tiffany is going to be so jelly."

"It's amazing." I peeked my head around the corner and looked at Foster. "Please tell me that I get one too."

He nodded with a big smile. "Of course."

Charlie showed me her bathroom, which was Jack and Jill, with one of the other bedrooms. It was turquoise, which was perfect and went with the pale blue in the bedroom.

As we walked down the hall peeking in doors, Foster gave me the rundown on how the house had recently been renovated, and the seller was looking for a quick close. We could move in as soon as we wanted.

I was beyond excited, and I hadn't even seen half the house.

"Sold." It was all that came out of my mouth as I walked into the master bedroom. It was huge with windows everywhere, just like in Charlie's room. It was painted a soft yellow with a beautiful coffered ceiling. It was even big enough for a complete sitting area. The en-suite bathroom had a tub I could swim in with a separate shower and his and her sinks, but the closets—that's right, plural—were the icing on the cake. I wouldn't have to share. I would have my own.

Foster came up from behind and wrapped his arms around me as I looked out over the vast property. "Sold, huh? You don't want to see the rest of the house first?"

"Of course, I want to see it, but I'm sure I will love it."

We stared out the windows together. "How big is the property?"

"Just over five acres. It's so peaceful out there that you'd never know that we're less than six miles to a Target." He kissed the top of my head. "Can't you just picture all the dogs running around out there?"

"And my pony?" Charlie's voice came from behind us.

I turned to find her standing in the doorway with her hands on her hips. "Pony?" My brow furrowed. When did that happen?

Foster stepped between us. "Hey, I said I would discuss that with your mother. The only promise was the dogs."

"She blew out a breath. "Fine. You said I get to pick five dogs, though, right?"

Foster nodded and shrugged when I cocked a brow at him in question.

"Okay, cool, but we're going to talk about this pony thing because we can't let that barn go to waste." She was such a sassy little thing, but I thought I'd leave this one up to Foster. I had no clue about animals and seeing that he had grown up on a farm, he knew way more than I did.

"We better get looking at the main floor so I can get my beautiful bride back to our wedding." Foster took my hand and led me down the stairs.

Charlie went outside to explore while we looked around.

Everything was done to perfection. The kitchen was something out of a magazine with my favorite part being the windows again. It seemed to be the main feature in the entire house.

Suddenly it dawned on me. "Can we even afford this place?" I'd been so caught up in how stunning everything was that I'd gotten ahead of myself.

"It looks more expensive than it is. I promise." His evasive answer had me a little concerned. "Don't worry, baby." He pulled me into his arms. "We can more than afford it."

"I trust you." I kissed his lips. "You did well. This place is everything I would've ever dreamed of."

His smile was bright. "I'm so glad. I'll call the agent on the drive back. I can't wait to grow old with you here."

I didn't want to leave, but we had a wedding to get back to. Foster called the agent and had them start the process on the house. He asked for the quickest closing possible. The biggest bonus was that Charlie didn't even have to change schools, and she would be able to take a bus.

Charlie took off in the hall before us while we waited for our cue. They announced Mr. and Mrs. Montgomery, and it made my insides giddy.

We went straight for the dance floor for our first dance as husband and wife. The song "You Are" by Lionel Richie started to play over the speakers. I melted into his arms as we swayed to the beat in our own little world.

After dinner, the speeches started. Our parents kicked them off, followed by Foster's best man.

When Charlie got up next, I was shocked since she wasn't much for public speaking like me.

"I don't have much to say except that I'm glad my mom has you, Foster. You really make her happy, and I like you too. But please don't have any babies. You're too old for that." The crowd all laughed when she came over to hug us both.

Foster and I hadn't talked much about kids, but I think we were good with Charlie's request. Foster squeezed my thigh under the table. "I think we'll have our hands full with her and all the animals she's going to talk me into bringing home."

I kissed his cheek. "I think you're right about that."

Dana got up next, and I could already see the tears shimmering in her eyes. She turned to us. "I still can't believe that my brother and my best friend got married today. I have to admit that I was shocked when I found out you'd been involved at all. I always thought you two hated each other. I don't know how I missed all the signs, but I'm sure glad you guys found your way back to each other again. Thank you, Foster, for giving me the greatest gift ever—a sister." She started to walk away but then went back to the microphone. "One more thing. You bet your ass that Wednesday girls' night is not going anywhere, either, so you better have a spare room for me."

I stood and hugged my best friend, who I now got to call my sister. "I love you, girl."

"Love you too. Don't let my brother give you any shit."

"I definitely won't."

Todd stood up next. "I'm going to keep this short. Foster, good luck." And that was it.

I slapped his ass as he pretended he was just going to walk right by us, and he stopped and leaned down to hug us both as he laughed before heading back to his seat.

We danced the night away, enjoying the love and company of our friends and family.

The End

EPILOGUE

DANA LOOKED around Starbucks and sat down before blowing out a harsh breath. "I honestly think you dodged a bullet."

"Me too, but I can't help but be a little sad. Mostly for Foster." It'd been a few days since we had a pregnancy scare, but it was still fresh in my mind. We were in our forties, and Charlie was going to be in high school soon. We were in no place to have kids.

She scrunched up her brow in confusion. "How so?"

"Because he doesn't have any kids of his own." I shrugged.

"And I already told you, baby, I'm perfectly content with that." Foster handed us our coffees and sat down beside me. "I love Charlie like she's mine, and between work and taking care of all of the animals, we don't have time for a baby." He kissed my cheek. "I love being able to have you guys all to myself; that wouldn't happen with an infant."

"I know you say that. I just felt sad—"

He interrupted before I could continue, "Kamryn, I wouldn't lie to you. If I truly wanted to have a baby, I would tell you. That's not something I'd be able to keep hidden." He was sincere; his eyes never seemed to lie. "And when Charlie's grown, we will get to enjoy grandkids. I hear that's even better than having kids."

"Whoa. Slow down there, buddy, Charlie's just a baby herself."

He chuckled but pacified me. "I didn't mean today, but one day in the far-off future."

"Thank you."

Dana took a sip of her coffee and set it down beside her. "So, what time do you have to be at Bucky's?"

I couldn't believe we were doing this. "In a few hours, but we should be leaving in about twenty minutes. We have to pick up the trailer, and then it'll take us around two hours to get over there."

"I can't wait to see Charlie's face when she gets home from school." Foster was probably just as excited as Charlie was going to be.

We'd found a pair of bonded large ponies for sale, and they were way too cute to pass up. The owner was selling his farm for financial reasons, and we got them for a steal. We'd had them vet checked last week and took a few days to get everything we needed and make sure all the fencing was secure. Foster had assured me over and over that he would make sure that Charlie stayed on top of her schoolwork and dance but that she would be responsible for a lot of the horse duties as well.

She had no idea this was coming. We'd talked about it a lot since the wedding, and I hadn't quite given a definitive answer, but when I stumbled on these posted in a Facebook group, it was love at first sight. They were adorable.

"You better take a video of that since I won't be there to see it. Foster used to ride all the time, so he will be a great coach for Charlie to learn with."

"We will. No way am I missing that one on camera."

We finished our coffees as we caught up on each other's lives before we headed out.

We got back to the house with thirty minutes to spare before Charlie got home. We got them both situated in the barn and attached the giant bows I'd bought to the front of their stalls. Foster parked the horse trailer on the far side of the house so Charlie wouldn't see it.

I texted Charlie to let her know we needed her out back when she got home to help with chicken feed, which we kept in the barn storage.

She walked around the corner, looking down at her phone, not even paying attention to her surroundings. She nearly walked right past the ponies except one of them snorted, and she stopped in her tracks. Charlie slowly turned to her left, and her mouth hung open in shock as her backpack dropped to the ground. She was speechless. She didn't move and say anything. She just stared between the two of them, and then a tear slipped down her cheek.

"Aren't you going to say something?" I was holding the camera, waiting with bated breath.

She turned her head and then smiled before running to Foster. She jumped into his arms and said *thank you* over and over.

"Hey, what am I? Chopped liver?" My daughter was a traitor.

"Sorry, thank you, Mom." She hugged me and kissed my cheek. "But, I figured this was more Foster than you."

"Actually, your mom was the one who found them." Foster threw me a bone.

Charlie went back over and petted them both on their noses. "What are their names?"

"Peanut Butter and Cookie." I thought they were the cutest names ever, so I hoped she didn't want to change them.

"You're kidding? Those are adorable. When do I get to ride them?"

"Slow down there, missy. You have a lot to learn before you get to ride. These two are going to be a huge responsibility for you, and you need to get to know them before you can ride." Foster knew what he was talking about, and I trusted him to keep her safe.

She rolled her eyes. "Ugh! When do we start *learning* then?"

Foster picked up her backpack and handed it to her. "Right after you finish your homework."

THE END

Don't miss out on news from

Kristie Leigh

Scan here to sign up

ACKNOWLEDGMENTS

Foster was the first book I ever attempted to write. I started writing it back in May 2015. I wrote 1,000 words and didn't pick it up again for about a year. Crazy right? He was supposed to be the first in a series of books, so in 2018 with the help of a "friend," I finished him and went on to start the next book, but I could never finish the others because Foster was always it for Kamryn in my mind. So, at the end of 2019, I decided to give them their HEA and finally finished their story.

Although this won't be my debut release, this will forever be my first book baby.

For those who know me, they will see a lot of myself in Kamryn, she's awesome, of course ;) And Emma in Charlie. Especially the snark!

I want to start by saying I'm a total flake, so I'm positive that I will forget people. So I apologize now if I do!

To my 3 kids, **Calum, Emma-Leigh** & **Tyler** who aren't EVER allowed to read this book, I love you more than life itself, even though you drive me batshit crazy <3

Chris, my poor husband, as you can imagine, I'm very hard to live with, and he puts up with A LOT of shit from me. We just celebrated 23 years together this year, he's been stuck with me since I was 16. I know, I will start a GoFundMe page for your donations to help him through all the hours of therapy <3

Aunty Gina, thank you for always being there for me and supporting me no matter how badly I fuck up. I love you to death <3 #missyouguys

Stephie, we've been through a fuckton in our friendship, but I couldn't imagine doing it with anyone else. You're the bestest bestie a girl could ever ask for, and I can't wait for what life throws at us next. It's never a dull moment for Mila Hart. I'll always be your pantiless whore bestie. Love you <3 #throughthickandthin

Phil, if you hadn't bought me that paperwhite, I don't think I would have ever gotten into books like I have. Thank you for listening to my ramblings about my books and giving your opinion on everything <3 #missyouguystoo

Dana, I don't even know where to begin, you're one of my best friends, thank fuck for that Book Bash ticket. You took me into your folds HAHA and welcomed me into Rehab with open arms. I couldn't imagine my life without you in it. You're my cheerleader, thank you for always being there for me <3 #gingersisters #BBF4ever

Jessi, my amazing personal support system, I will be forever grateful that I found you, you've become such a big part of my life, and I'm so lucky to still have you in it while you head off on your own journey outside the coaching world. Love you girl <3 #amwritingjessi #bestauthorcoachever

To **Dayna**, **Jennifer**, **Judy**, & **Shayne,** for taking the time to read everything and anything, your feedback and encouragement were amazing, and I will forever be grateful. Love you all <3

Patti, thank you for everything. You have been there for me from day one, cheering me on, encouraging me—I couldn't have done this without you <3

Heather C. Leigh without you, Todd wouldn't exist, and he's been one of my fave characters to write. Thank you for being such a great friend <3

Krystal, he's finally done! Can you even believe it?

Thank you for loving Foster as much as I do and pushing for more. Without you, I don't think Foster would have his HEA <3

To the narcissistic "friend," you may no longer be a part of my life in *any* way, but I will always cherish my time with the old you. I also wouldn't feel right without giving you credit for helping me with the OG Foster. I also have to thank you for pushing me and my bestie together. Without you, we would not be as thick as thieves, and for that, I am forever grateful; she's the best gift you ever gave me.

With love and gratitude,

Kristie Leigh
xoxo

PLAYLIST

Every story needs a killer playlist, and this series is no exception. These songs? They've got all the angst, heat, and chaos that come with second chances, bad decisions, and late-night confessions.

🎵 **Sugar Sugar** – The Archies

🎵 **What Do You Mean?** – Justin Bieber

🎵 **Lucky You** – Eminem

🎵 **Body Like A Back Road** – Sam Hunt

🎵 **Sorry Not Sorry** – Demi Lovato

🎵 **Chains** – Nick Jonas

🎵 **Woman** – Kesha

Scan or click the QR code for the full playlist and let the drama play on. 😊🎶

Kristie Leigh is a fiery redhead and USA Today Bestselling Author who fell in love with small-town life long before she ever experienced it. Growing up, she dreamed of quiet streets, friendly neighbors, and the kind of close-knit community that feels like home. Now, she's living that dream in a rural Alabama town with her high school sweetheart and their three kids.

Her passion for small-town romance comes alive in her stories, where back roads and burning hearts lead to love, second chances, and the kind of happily-ever-afters that stay with you long after the last page.

Discover more about

Kristie Leigh